WHITE RAVENS

OWEN SHEERS

WHITE RAVENS

NEW STORIES FROM THE
MABINOGION

SEREN

Seren is the book imprint of
Poetry Wales Press Ltd
57 Nolton Street, Bridgend, Wales, CF31 3AE
www.seren-books.com

ISBN 978-1-85411-503-4

A CIP record for this title is available from the British Library.

Cover design by Mathew Bevan

Inner design and typesetting by books@lloydrobson.com

The publisher acknowledges the financial support of the
Welsh Books Council.

Contents

I fy Nheidiau

New Stories from the Mabinogion

Introduction

Some stories, it seems, just keep on going. Whatever you do to them, the words are still whispered abroad, a whistle in the reeds, a bird's song in your ear.

Every culture has its myths; many share ingredients with each other. Stir the pot, retell the tale and you draw out something new, a new flavour, a new meaning maybe. There's no one right version. Perhaps it's because myths were a way of describing our place in the world, of putting people and their search for meaning in a bigger picture that they linger in our imagination.

The eleven stories of the *Mabinogion* ('story of youth') are diverse native Welsh tales taken from two medieval manuscripts. But their roots go back hundreds of years, through written fragments and the unwritten, storytelling tradition. They were first collected under this title, and translated into English, in the nineteenth century.

The *Mabinogion* brings us Celtic mythology, Arthurian romance, and a history of the Island of Britain seen through the eyes of medieval Wales – but tells tales that stretch way beyond the boundaries of contemporary Wales, just as the 'Welsh' part of this island once did: Welsh was once spoken as far north as Edinburgh. In one tale, the gigantic Bendigeidfran wears the crown of London, and his severed head is buried there, facing France, to protect the land from invaders.

There is enchantment and shape-shifting, conflict, peacemaking, love, betrayal. A wife conjured out of flowers is punished for unfaithfulness by being turned into an owl, Arthur and his knights chase a magical wild boar and its piglets from Ireland across south Wales to Cornwall, a prince changes places with the king of the underworld for a year...

Many of these myths are familiar in Wales, and some have filtered through into the wider British tradition, but others are little known beyond the Welsh border. In this series of New Stories from the Mabinogion the old tales are at the heart of the new, to be enjoyed wherever they are read.

Each author has chosen a story to reinvent and retell for their own reasons and in their own way: creating fresh, contemporary tales that speak to us as much of the world we know now as of times long gone.

Penny Thomas, series editor

'He who is a leader; let him be a bridge'

Bendigeidfran, Branwen, Daughter of Llyr

White Ravens

Rhian

Let me tell you something. If you wanted to curse someone, I don't know why you would, but if you did, if you wanted to make their life hard, if you wanted to leave them as vulnerable to grief as possible, I reckon you could do a lot worse than make them a woman in a house of men. Not everyone will agree, I know, but that's how I was feeling the morning when all this happened. After what I'd seen the night before, this was the thought rattling round my head when that old man came tottering up the path to sit down next to me.

I'd been sitting on a bench by the Tower for a good hour by then, watching the sun come up, turning the Thames gold before rising and dulling it back to brown. I was still staring at the river, watching its currents swirl round the bridge struts, when I caught sight of him out the corner of my eye. He was making his way up the path, slowly, an old man in a tweed suit. Tall once probably, but stooped over now, leaning heavily on a stick at every second step. I knew right away he was going to sit down next to me, even as I saw him walking up the path. It was like he was coming for me from the off, not just passing. But like I said, I had other things on my mind. Like curses, my bloody brothers and what the hell I was going to do now? Alone in London for the first time in my life, hundreds of miles from home and a thousand quid in used notes in my pocket. Those notes did give me some options at least. But it wasn't options I was short of at that point. It was something else. Ideas, a direction; a compass for the new circumstances I'd gone and put myself in.

I'd been living with my brothers on the farm for ten years by then, so believe me I knew what I was talking about when I came up with that curse. We'd been a proper family once, but for those last ten years, all through my early twenties, it had been just them and me. Just Dewi, four years older, Sion, two years younger, and me in the middle, up there on the mountain with the wind and the rain, with the buzzards and the ravens. Proper ravens mind, not like those being fed in the grounds of the Tower that morning; hopping round some ponced-up Beefeater chucking them scraps of meat. No, our ravens went looking for their own carrion; big bloody black rags of birds, coughing and corkscrewing into the air above our tumbledown farm, so old and crooked you couldn't tell if it'd been built on the hillside or just grown from out of it.

My father was the first to go, when I was six years old. He left my mother with that farm, a thousand or so sheep, a swelling egg of a bruise round her right eye, and the colour of his own in the eyes of us three scrawny kids. 'Blue as a summer's sky' is what he used to say when he held our faces and looked into them, '*Fel glesni'r awyr ar bnawn o haf*'. Ten years after he left us it was Mam's turn to go, carried out of our front porch on the shoulders of four farmers she'd never spoken to beyond a nod and none who'd ever done what their own wives had kept telling them to do and taken my father aside for a good talking to.

I was sixteen when Mam died, just old enough not to be taken away. Sometimes I wish I had been though, instead of being left with Dewi and Sion. Not that they've ever done me any wrong, as such. They're Dad's sons but they haven't taken after him in every way. No, not every way. It's just that, well, so far they've never really done me any right either.

You'd think I'd have better memories of my father than I do, but I don't. Just snapshots, stray photos come loose from some album I've tucked away in my head out of sight. Riding on his shoulders when he went out to check on the flock – that's one of them. I used to warm my hands down the back of his collar while he held me on, his fingers meeting round my thin ankles. Sliding on a feed bag filled with straw down the back field after a snowfall, that's another. And the sound he used to make when working the dogs, I'll never forget that. Like a shout he'd swallowed trying to escape, but going deep into his ribs instead. Still loud enough, somehow, for the dogs to hear him. Sometimes I still catch his smell on the clothes of my brothers. A mix of soil, sheep nuts, hay, hill-wind and soap. I know you'll say wind hasn't got a smell, but I swear up there it has. Mineral it is. Or steel. You can taste it, not like in London. Christ, I soon learnt about the air there didn't I? Sucking in great gobfuls of the stuff, all fumes and God knows what else, as I sat on that bench, sobbing my eyes out 'til my heart was right up in my throat.

The best memory I've got of my father isn't a smell though, or a sight, but a touch. He had this scar, you see, a burn all over his right hand and running up his arm as far as his elbow. Some accident as a kid was all he ever said. When I was little, four, five years old, I used to fall asleep on his lap beside the fire, stroking my fingers up and down that scar. I'd feel the coolness of it, hairless and smooth, knotting all the way up his forearm. When I touched it with my eyes shut I'd see those swirls of colour you get inside marbles.

I used to think it funny a scar could feel so nice, and that it was strange how beautiful it looked in the light of the same thing that had made it in the first place.

After Dad left us, once they were old enough, my brothers took over the running of the farm. Mam never seemed to miss him after he went, not openly anyway. She'd never known her own parents, so perhaps she was used to people only being there by not being there. We never heard her speak of Dad again from the day he walked out the door. Or of his father, our *Tad-cu*, who she'd always talked of fondly, with a smile we never saw her use for anyone else. His wife, Dad's Mam, had died giving birth to Dad, so *Tad-cu* had been the only relative we'd ever heard about. But after Dad left us, well, it was as if Mam's memory of *Tad-cu* went with him because she never spoke of him again either. It's funny, she used to tell us all the time our family had farmed these same hills for thousands of years, but did we know anything about who they were? Did we know their names, their faces? Not bloody likely, not a thing.

Once my brothers began taking on the farm work Mam threw herself into the running of the house and into making sure I wasn't going to stay in it a moment longer than I had to. That's how she'd wake me up on winter mornings to go catch the bus down in the village, with that idea in her head. 'How you ever going to get away from here girl?' she'd say, tugging the curtains back on the still dark day outside. 'If you don't get out of bed first? C'mon now *cariad*, up with you now.' She always said it softly mind, never harsh or anything. I knew even then all she wanted was better for me than she'd ever had herself. But then she went and died didn't she? Slipped on some ice out in the yard and hit her head. Within a week of burying her I was out of school and in the kitchen back home, cooking and cleaning and shopping for my brothers; looking after them so as they could look after me, that's how Dewi put it. And from then on that's how it was; that was us. The branches of our family tree, which had once spread all over these hills, cut back to just Dewi, Sion and me up on that bare slope with little hope of any new roots or growth in any direction. There was a time, early on, when Dewi and Sion used to go into town on the odd Saturday night, but they soon stopped that. Poor sods had no more idea how to handle the girls down there than they did a bloody giraffe. And as for me, well I'm sure they thought it was just brotherly protection, brotherly love even, but neither of them ever took too kindly to me getting friendly with another man. There were a few, over the years, and some even made it up to the farm. But, well, our lives had become different by then, and however much they wanted me – and I saw them want me mind, saw their eyes fair cook up in their sockets when they got a glimpse of my shape – I think in the end the way we lived scared them off. That and my brothers, hunched over the kitchen table, glowering from under their frowns and over their soups.

Pretty soon any friends I used to have in the village or down in the town left the area for jobs or college. Once they had, I suppose I let myself fall into our way of things up there. I'm sure the village talked, they always did, but Dewi and Sion had a pretty simple response to that too. 'Sod 'em,' they'd say over dinner. 'What do they know anyway? Bunch of bloody blow-ins.' That's how they were, see. Had some sense of bloody entitlement, up there on our high farm. No time for any family from 'down there' who'd only been around a couple of hundred years or so. Ridiculous. Though sometimes, when I'm out on the hill, or right up the top of the mountain, I can see their point, in a way. On some days, in the right weather, a hundred years does feel like nothing up there. Like no more than a lark's song on the wind compared to the memory of those hills them-selves, or of the rocks jutting out of them, like the battlements of some buried castle.

So, like I said, that was us: the poor orphans on the hill. We worked by day, and at night we ate, listened to Mam's old rock 'n' roll tapes or watched reality TV shows about people who lived on a different planet to us, not just in a different world. Skinny American heiresses, botoxed soap actors stuck in a house together or a bunch of right annoying twats on a desert island somewhere. But you know what? We might have been alright in the end. Maybe, just maybe I wouldn't have ended up thinking that curse about men and women was such a good one after all. Who knows? We might even have been happy, in the end. Or at least, not unhappy; if only those men hadn't come.

But they did come didn't they? All decked out in their white spaceman suits like those scientists in ET who sealed up the kid's house he was hiding in. And when they came they killed our whole flock, over a thousand grazing ewes and lambs. Just four of them there were, standing in the front paddock with rifles at their shoulders, shooting ewe after ewe, lamb after lamb, dropping them all with a single shot each. Then they'd reload and shoot again. And again. And again, with the three of us standing there like we'd had our own brains blown out, unbelieving it was happening, wide-eyed and watching it all.

It was Sion who'd seen the blisters first, on a ewe's tongue lolling out the side of her mouth. She was feeding a couple of lambs and every time they gave her an extra hard jab with their heads a big old dab of foam and saliva would drop from her lips onto the grass. We thought we'd escaped the outbreak, but obviously we hadn't. It had been spreading for a month by then. The first report had come from Devon and within a few weeks there were Foot and Mouth cases as far north as Cumbria. We'd had no movement of stock, in or out, from the farm, and no visitors either. We'd driven into town of course, but from the day of that first report Dewi had laid a strip of straw soaked with disinfectant across the gateway. Every time we came back he'd spray the wheels of the pick-up too, so, yes, we thought we'd escaped. But that foam and those blisters, big as bloody bubble wrap, well, they told a different story.

The inspector came the next day, casting a right old frown over the state of the place as we walked him though the yard to where we'd penned the flock in the paddock. To be fair, when I saw the farm through his eyes I could see his point: the rusted skeleton of a tractor sunk in the ground, the loose slates on the roof, the tyres piled up the side of the house. No fault with the sheep themselves though, he had to admit that. Apart from the obvious, of course. 'Fine animals, fine animals,' he'd muttered to himself as he looked them over, already calculating in his head, no doubt, how long and how many men he'd need to kill them all.

The men in the spacesuits came the next day. When they'd done their shooting they piled the carcases in the paddock, right there in front of the house, doused them with petrol then set them alight. The bodies took with a roar, like some angered god it was. A raging pyre of legs and heads and popping eyes that lit up the windows of the farm the way sunsets always have. They must have seen that smoke stack for miles all around. A thick black pillar it was, right up to the clouds. And the smell, well, with the wind behind it that must have travelled as far as the village at least.

The pyre was still burning when the men left at nightfall, after which it looked as if the farm itself was on fire, every window full of flames, like it was our lives in there, not the carcases outside, that were burning. Which of course, in a way, it was.

Everything changed after that. That was the end of it all. Or the beginning I suppose, seeing as it was those men and their shooting that led to me sitting on that bench by the Tower that morning. Sitting on that bench watching the sun come up, cursing my brothers and seeing that old man out the corner of my eye as he *stepped, sticked, stepped, sticked* up the path towards me.

When I looked out my window the day after the men came, there was just a long patch of smoking ashes left, a black and grey scar in the middle of the paddock. For the first time in hundreds of years the mountain behind our farm was quiet. Just the odd caw of a crow or a raven's cough, both of them probably wondering what had happened to all those weak lambs they'd been keeping their beady eyes on.

At that time of year the mountain should have been full of the bleating of new lambs and the calls of ewes answering them. Then, in a few months' time, there'd be a day and night of more urgent calls as those same ewes searched the hillside for the lambs we'd taken to market. But after the men in spacesuits there was none of that, nothing. That night, when the ashes had finally stopped smoking, I walked up onto the mountain, just to get out of the house and away from the anger of my brothers. I took a torch, sweeping it over the slope in front of me as I climbed. But all the beam caught was grass, grass, grass, not a single pair of green eyes, bright and hard in the light; not a single long black face rising from a ragged pile of wool. Just the night, briefly burnt away by the torch's beam, then washing back in again after it.

Looking back now I can see we lost a lot more than just those sheep that day. Something else got burnt in that fire; something else shrivelled up on itself, curled and blackened to a brittle crisp, and whatever it was, it lay deep in the hearts of my brothers.

Dewi blamed old Probert over the hill. There was good compensation to be had for losing your flock. Probert was well into his seventies with no sons of his own. So what interest would he have in keeping on farming? Dewi was convinced he'd infected his flock on purpose, then let them out on the hill.

'Old bastard,' he'd said as he kicked through those ashes in the paddock. 'How the bloody else did it come here?'

Whether it was Probert or not, Dewi's suspicion soon spread to Sion, as infectious as the disease itself. Between them they spread the blame too, out into the whole world, until that's where my brothers saw it lying – out there, in the hands of the world beyond our farm. They went cold, the two of them, because of what those men in their spacesuits had done to our flock, to our lives. That fire turned them to ice. Or at least, I hope that was the case. Otherwise what other excuse can I find for them, for what they did? What other reason could there be for them to have gone from tending sheep to stealing them, from being farmers to killers?

Step, Stick. Step, Stick.

Stop.

I waited for him to walk on but, like I said, I knew he wouldn't. I knew he was always heading for that bench, and for me.

I carried on looking at the river sliding its way through the city. As he sat down I felt his shadow flick over me, then the flex of the bench under my thighs as it took his weight. I kept on looking ahead, shifting my gaze to the ravens now. They'd finished their feeding and were taking up positions on the railings and lawns around the castle. Waiting for the tourists to come I guess; waiting to be gawped at, photographed and no doubt, when the Beefeaters weren't watching, fed again, slipped crusts of Costa Coffee sandwich and Starbucks muffin.

'They say they can tell your future you know.'

His voice caught me by surprise. There was no intake of breath, no shifting on the bench as he turned to me. Just suddenly his voice, clear and easy in the morning air. He didn't have an accent as such, more what Mam would have called 'educated'.

I didn't say anything, didn't look at him. I'd heard about London and seen enough on TV to know you didn't go talking to old blokes on benches. So I just kept looking at the ravens, running their big old beaks under their wings like they were sharpening them, then settling again to catch the day's first heat in their midnight wings.

'The ravens,' he continued. 'They say they can tell your future. Coracomancy they call it.' I thought he'd stopped then, but he repeated the last word, slowly and more quietly, like he was still getting used to it himself. 'Yes, coracomancy.'

Now he'd spoken a bit more I could hear the age in his voice, like something in his throat had come loose, making the edges of his words watery. I couldn't help sneaking a look at him then, just a quick sideways glimpse. When I did he was looking right back at me, bold as brass, so I snapped my head back round and stared down at the ravens in the Tower again. He carried on talking.

'You know the sort of thing, cawing to the right

means a journey will go well, picking up a stick or some other object... oh, yes, like that one there.' As if on command one of the ravens hopped over the lawn and picked up a twig. It stood there, the twig unwieldy in its beak, like a stupid dog that doesn't know what to do with a stick it's been thrown. 'Yes, well that,' he continued, 'that's supposed to mean something will be found.' He allowed himself a little chuckle then, like he'd said something right funny. 'Can't say I believe any of it myself. After all a man's got to understand his past before he can get a look at his future hasn't he?' He paused then, like he was waiting for me to reply. I didn't, and maybe that's why when he spoke to me again it was in a lower, softer tone that made me turn back to look at him. 'Or a woman of course,' he said. 'Or a woman.'

This time I held his stare. His eyes were milky blue, his hair bright white. He was clean shaven so you could still make out a once-strong face under the loose skin drooping round his cheekbones and under his chin. Now, it isn't like I haven't seen men look at me before. Like I said, the few I've known well enough to undress in front of haven't been able to hide a thing when they've got a proper sight of me. When I go into town for market too, I can walk down a street so as to collect men's eyes like burrs if I want to, so that when I reach the end I'm covered in eyeballs from the street behind me. But the look of this old fella, well, it wasn't like that. His look was just clear, honest I guess. Like he was drinking me in, but not in a seedy way. More like, well, like he was reading me.

'So,' he said, his voice still soft and low. 'What brings you to the Tower on such a lovely morning miss? What winds have blown you here today?'

And that was it. I don't know how he did it, but that one question, with his eyes looking into mine and asked in that voice, well, it exploded in my head it did. Just went off and undid me, bringing my heart jumping back into my throat and the tears back into my eyes. And all I could think of was I don't know, I don't know, I don't know. What had brought me there? It was a bloody good question, the same one I'd been asking myself all morning, ever since I'd left my brothers covered in blood in the back of that lorry.

After our flock was slaughtered, just like old Probert and everyone else, we got our compensation, fair and square. It was meant so as we could replace the flock. But my brothers had other ideas. After what had happened, and with them feeling hurt by the whole world, they had no interest in starting over again, in hauling their arses up the mountain three times a day to fetch back new sheep who had no sense of where they belonged bred into them. Well, I say they had other ideas, but the truth is it was Sion's friend, Lloyd down at the *Esso* garage who brought them. He knew some men in Bristol who'd set up a network of contacts in Birmingham, Manchester, even London. These men had asked if Lloyd could find someone to run the Welsh arm of their operation. They'd got the Lake District and the Pennines covered. But not Wales. Yet. Lloyd came up one night and talked Dewi and Sion through it all, and by the time he'd walked back out the door, leaving the back of an envelope scrawled with more zeros than my brothers were ever used to seeing, they'd agreed to be that Welsh arm.

To be honest, I didn't believe any of it. I knew my brothers and I didn't see how they were ever going to pull this one off. I thought it was a bit of bravado, a bit of pride-patching after the burning of our flock. But well, just goes to show doesn't it? People can surprise you, even if you think you know them better than you do yourself. Because, believe me, my brothers didn't just pull it off, they went for it wholesale: lock, stock.

They spent our compensation on a large horse lorry which, with the help of Lloyd, they converted to their needs. First I knew of that bloody great thing was when it came lumbering up our track to block all the light into the house. And that's where it stayed too, parked there for the next fortnight, casting a shadow over the farm as they hammered sheets of metal over its side windows, sound proofed its insides and put in a second, reinforced floor.

While Sion and Lloyd worked on the lorry Dewi

got himself a part-time job in the abattoir in town. On weekends and nights he'd pass on what he'd learnt to Sion and tell him what tools they needed to buy. Then one morning that September them towers came down in America and suddenly the whole world seemed to be shifting on its axis. Everything seemed darker, and yet somehow new too, so in a way what my brothers were doing began to feel in rhythm with the times. That's what I told myself anyway.

The next spring, just when the lowland lambs were being born, Lloyd at the *Esso* got his HGV licence and less than a year after those men in spacesuits, when the first buttercups and daisies were just starting to push through that old ash scar in the paddock, my brothers were ready to start.

The plan was bold but simple, which is probably why, to start with, it all worked so well. The day before a job my brothers would sharpen their knives and take a good long nap. Lloyd would come up around ten and the three of them would leave the farm around eleven, Lloyd driving and my brothers riding shotgun with a couple of collies at their feet. Within a few hours they'd be at the field of some other farm, far enough away for them not to be known. Using the dogs they'd round up as many lambs and sheep as the lorry could take – around 100 in all – lock them in, and go. Lloyd would head for the nearest motorway and Dewi and Sion would get to work in the back, slaughtering the sheep.

It was hard, bloody work, but they got right quick at it. A few hours later, at four or five in the morning, the lorry would pull up at the kitchen doors of restaurants, at the service lifts of hotels, and Lloyd would hand over prime cuts of Welsh lamb so fresh the customers could still feel the animal's living heat pressing into their hands through the plastic it was wrapped in. In return Lloyd would leave each back door with a tidy sum of used notes in brown envelopes. If all went well Dewi and Sion, after they'd dropped Lloyd off, could be back home by eight or nine the next morning.

The best job by far was London. Think about it. How much do you pay for a good bit of lamb in those smart hotel restaurants, or in one of those TV chef bistros? Thirty, forty quid for a shoulder? Well, a sheep's got two of those hasn't it? Hundred sheep at forty quid a shoulder, that's 8,000 quid for a start. And that's just the shoulders. Not that Dewi and Sion ever took home that much. After they'd under-cut the local suppliers by more than half, paid Lloyd, given the men in Bristol their cut, taken in fuel costs and the rest, well, they might bring back between ten or fifteen grand from one job. Still, a bloody sight more than they'd ever got from farming their own stock. And those places in London? Well, they couldn't get enough of the stuff. No one seemed to care where the meat came from, least of all the lucky bugger who got to eat it.

And what about me? Well, I suppose I was happy to be as blind as those London diners. I'd take the money my brothers brought home, stick a chunk of it in a drawer and use the rest for that month's shopping and bills. Then I'd try to forget about where it all came from, heading into the kitchen sharpish to cook up breakfast and get away from the sound of Sion hosing down the lorry. Hose it for hours he would until the gutters in the yard ran red all afternoon.

God knows what we were going to do with the money. I had my own plans. Go to college, move to Cardiff; get some job in an office with big windows looking over the bay. Sion did, once, bring back some holiday brochures from town. He'd sat there at the kitchen table, flicking through all the bright skies, white beaches and women in bikinis while the rain hammered at the window and the wind got its fingers under the slates. All that brightness and gloss though, I think it seemed too impossible for him, sitting there in our dark kitchen, because he never picked up that brochure again. The next time I saw it, Dewi was using a page to light the fire; a woman's head, all smiles against a palm tree, rumpled out the side of his fist as he shoved her under a log and lit a match to her blue, blue sky.

It all went pretty smoothly though. They never did too many jobs, and never any too close together. So, again, maybe we'd have been alright, even after the spacesuit men. Maybe we'd have made it all work, if only Lloyd hadn't gone and come down with the shits like he did, and if Dewi and Sion hadn't come and asked me to drive them instead.

'Who else we gonna ask?' Dewi said that night, standing over me at the kitchen table. 'There's no one else, is there Rhi? No one else knows.'

Sion didn't say a thing, just skulked around the sink, looking out the window then went to tinker with the lorry and give the dogs some water. Dewi put a hand on my shoulder. 'Please Rhi,' he said softly, like he was talking down a nervous foal. 'Jus' this once?'

'I've never driven that thing Dewi,' I said, not looking at him. 'An' never driven to London at all.'

'No, but that's it, see?' he said, excited as a kid at Christmas. He pulled up a chair beside me. 'Lloyd's put the whole job on this.' He took out a chunky bit of plastic with a screen in it. 'The route into London an' all the drop-offs. All you gotta do is follow the arrows an' listen to the voice. That's it Rhi. We'll be back by morning you know we will. Jus' follow the voice, tha's all.'

I picked up the Sat Nav from the table and turned it over in my hand. I thought of all that cash in the drawer in the dresser. I thought of Mam, waking me up in the mornings – 'how you ever going to get anywhere girl, if you don't leave this place first?' I thought of seeing London at dawn, of an office in the bay with floor-to-ceiling windows, of sitting in a lecture hall taking notes. I thought of meeting a man who'd know how to talk to me, how to hold me and touch me. I thought of that pyre, the men in spacesuits, the buttercups pushing through ash. I thought of all that and when I did, I said yes. I said yes, trying not to think about what would happen in the back of that old horse lorry, in just a few hours time, somewhere on a motorway between here and London.

I'll say this for my brothers, they'd got right quick at it I'm telling you. They worked those dogs better at night than my dad ever did by day. Not that I saw the actual rustling or anything. No, I stayed in the cab. I just felt it and heard it. Heard the clatter of hooves on the ramp; felt the shiver of their running weight down the length of the lorry. Heard the confused bleating, the stamping of their feet and saw in my mind's eye their heads, stretching over each other's rumps, their slit nostrils, flaring and panting, their eyes wide and their pink tongues showing with each tremulous baa. Then all of a sudden the passenger door was opening and the dogs were jumping in, their own tongues lolling out their mouths, right excited by it all. Then it was closing again and Dewi was banging on the side of the lorry, telling me to get on out of there. I shifted the gear-stick to first and eased that bloody great thing out of the field, burning bright green on the Sat Nav stuck on the windshield. And then, as I trundled down the lane, lights off, she spoke to me. A right posh woman, like Joanna Lumley. 'At the end of the road, turn right,' she said. 'Turn right.' And that was it, we were on our way; Dick Whittington, off to London to see the queen.

Picture it if you can. It's 2am somewhere on the M4 between Swindon and Reading. The tarmac ahead is patched with smudges of light from the tallest streetlamps I've ever seen. The darkness beyond them is pricked with the tail-lights of other lorries still on the road at this hour. The steering wheel of mine feels strong and secure under my hands, the beams of its headlights eating up the road with weighty ease. I've got the radio on, full volume, not that the dogs seem to notice, flat out in the footwell. The embankments slide past me on either side, scattered with puny saplings planted in circles of plastic. Every thirty miles or so a services looms up out of the night, an oasis of light and menus, then fades away again in my wing mirrors. Eventually, in the distance, London begins to rise on the horizon. It's the first time I've ever seen the city. At first it looks scrappy as hell, but as the towers get taller and the traffic flowing between them thicker, it begins to cast a spell on me. But even that does nothing to shake the cold sweat that's been gripping me all the way. Because all this time, while I've been looking forward, I haven't been able to block out what's happening a few metres behind my head – my brothers, Dewi and Sion speed-slaughtering and butchering

100 head of stolen lambs and ewes.

I try to focus on the city enveloping me, on this feeling of sliding smoothly along the thread of the road, deeper and deeper into its complicated knot. And I focus, too, on the disembodied voice of the woman, on Joanna's plummy diction, guiding me into London, taking me further and further away from Wales, home and my usual bearings. 'In 400 yards, turn left. Turn left.'

I have to say, 'listen to her' because I did, but I had to question her priorities at times. 'Attention, speed camera ahead,' she'd whisper in my ear. 'Fifty yards, 40, 30, 20…' Speed camera? Christ love, I couldn't help thinking, that's the least of our worries right now. Try 'Attention, illegal butchering of stolen stock' for size. 'Twenty, 30, 40, 50. At the next junction, turn yourself in. Turn yourself in.' That would be more like it.

But of course, we didn't did we? No, we went ahead with it all just as planned and you know what? It went just as planned too, nice and smooth, just as Dewi had said it would. Until the very last drop-off.

Which is when it all went very wrong indeed.

Apart from me, it was clear everyone else had done this before. The chefs at the kitchen doors, the Polish dishwashers who lugged the meat from the lorry, the pooled blood shape-shifting at the bottom of the plastic bags like clouds on a sped-up weather forecast. And of course my brothers, passing that meat out through the barely opened back door of the lorry. All I had to do was pull up where Joanna told me – 'You have reached your second destination' – and collect the money from the chef once he'd inspected the meat. After the first time I began to relax. By the fourth I was even beginning to enjoy it a little. I can't lie; it all began to excite me. Sitting in the warm fug of the lorry's cab, thumbing through wads of cash as London bruised up through an early morning lit in all the right places. A couple of thumps from Dewi on the side of the lorry and I'd start up and drive on again, waiting for Joanna to tell me where to go. 'At the next junction turn right. Turn right.'

We did the last drop-off exactly on schedule, at

around 5am, just in time to leave the city before the traffic got heavy. And that should have been it. I should have just waited for Dewi's thump on the side of the lorry, and driven on home. But I didn't did I?

I don't know what it was, but having all that cash up front, having got through the night, got through London, having *seen* London, I wanted to share it all with Dewi and Sion. I wanted them to see the money, to hold it, to know the reward for their night's labour. So instead of waiting for Dewi's thump I went on round to the back of the lorry and gave the door a little tap of my own. It cracked open and there was Dewi's eye, looking at me.

'What is it Rhi? Everythin' alright?' He sounded tired, worn out, and I felt a sudden flood of tenderness towards him.

'Yeah, everything's fine Dew. Jus' wanted to give you the cash in there. You know, so you can check it an' all. Probably safer then me having it up front don't you think?'

We were in a little alley behind one of those famous hotels, with the lorry reversed in so there was just a wall behind me. They'd used it before and knew the CCTV camera on the corner was knackered. The chef had seen to that months ago. Dewi popped his head out further and I saw a big smear of blood across his cheek where he must have wiped his face with his hand. He did a quick scope, just in case, then gave a jerk of his head. 'Yeah, alright,' he said, eyeing the fat envelope in my hand. Swinging the door wider he sat down on the tailgate and took it from me. Which is when I saw the full state of him, head to toe in blood, and of the lorry behind him too, lit by a single bulb hanging from the ceiling.

'Jesus,' I heard Dewi say as he thumbed through the notes. 'Bloody hell, look at that will you?' Which is exactly what I was thinking, but in a very different way. Dewi was spellbound, as he was more and more those days, by the sight of that money; of all that potential for things and happening held in his hand. But me? Well, I was just knocked for six by the sight of that lorry. Christ, bloody hell indeed. Now I understood why Sion hosed it down for hours after. Growing up on the farm it wasn't like I hadn't seen my fair share of slaughtering. But this was different. There was blood everywhere. On the ceiling, up the sides, in big puddles on the floor. The stink of it hit me in a slow wave; a rich, iron smell wafting out into the alley like a rotten memory of tougher times in the city. Over Dewi's shoulder I could make out a large bin. It was overflowing with hooves and heads. There were a couple of bags beside it, full of entrails. Sion lay next to them, knackered out, slumped against the bloody wall like the last survivor of some ancient massacre. And then, as if all this wasn't bad enough, after he'd handed the first thousand back to me, each note imprinted with a fainter and fainter bloody thumbprint, Dewi swivelled on his haunches and wagged a wad of cash at Sion. And Sion, my little brother who'd once cried when Dad said he couldn't have a pony, lit up with a big old grin, bright as those holiday-brochure smiles, in the middle of his blood-washed face.

I walked away. Just like that. Didn't think about it, didn't even know I was doing it. But I did, just walked away from it all, from the lorry, the smell, the wad of cash and from my bloody brothers, unbelieving that all our family had come to was this. That all our generations of farmers, of men and women who'd reared animals on that high hill had trickled down to the sorry sight of the three of us counting out bad money in a blood-soaked lorry in a back alley in London before dawn.

I didn't know where I was going. I just walked and walked. Dewi must have thought I was going back to the cab, because I never heard him call for me. In walking away like that I'd completely screwed them of course. Neither of them was in any state to drive, up all night killing and butchering, and neither were any sight for a passing policeman either. So yes, I'd screwed them over good and proper, leaving like that. But I didn't care. I never wanted to see them again. I never wanted to see them because of what they'd done, because of the turn they'd chosen all those months ago and because of how they'd gone and dragged me along with them. Not just that night either, but always. Because okay, that might have been the first time I'd seen inside the back of the lorry after a night's job, but hadn't I always taken the money that came from it? Hadn't I always stashed it in that drawer and used it to buy the food I ate, to fuel my dreams of the future? Of course I had and I reckon that's why I didn't stop walking for a good two hours. Because I wasn't just trying to get away from my brothers was I? Oh no, I was trying to get away from myself too, and I knew, when I finally sat down on that bench by the Tower, crying my bloody eyes out, that there wasn't much chance of me doing that now was there?

'I don't know... I don't know.'

This was the best I could manage. When the old man looked me in the eye and asked me what had brought me to the Tower, that's all I could say. I mean, I couldn't exactly tell him what I just told you could I? But it was true as well. I didn't know. Like he'd said, you've got to understand your past before you can tell your future, and right then on that bench, that morning, I sure as hell didn't understand a thing about mine.

When I told him I didn't know he turned away from me, real slow like, and I thought I'd somehow disappointed him. Suddenly, though I'd only just met him, I wanted him to turn back, to look at me again with those milky eyes and tell me it was alright, that it was alright to not have a bloody clue where you're going or where you've been. But he didn't; he just rested both his hands on his walking stick and his chin on his hands and looked out over the river to the city, hazy on the other side. Eventually he let out a sigh and, dipping a hand into his waistcoat, pulled out a silver pocket watch on a chain. He looked down at its face, not so much as to tell the time, but more as if he was looking through it, not at it, like it was a porthole not a watch, showing him a view of elsewhere, somewhere far away. He was still looking at it when he spoke to me again.

'Would you like to hear a story?' he said, still speaking soft and low.

I sniffed back my tears. Maybe he was a nutter after all, I thought. But I wanted to hear him speak again, so I answered him. 'What's it about?' I said.

'Oh,' he said, still looking at the watch. 'Those ravens down there.'

I looked down at the birds around the Tower, strutting and preening on the fence posts and railings. 'Those ravens?'

'Well,' he said, putting the watch away and turning to me with a smile. 'Not those ravens exactly, no. But their ancestors, yes.'

'Their ancestors?'

'Yes.' He was enjoying this now, the smile putting a shine in his eye.

'I don't know,' I said. 'I haven't really got time for a story.'

It was true. I'd just left my brothers covered in blood, in the back of a lorry in a back alley behind a hotel. Not really the time for stories.

'Oh, come now,' he said, looking at me from under a mock frown. 'There's always time for a story.'

I sighed, good and heavy, and when I did it felt like a lump of lead melting inside me. Maybe he was right. Maybe I could stay for a bit. The sun was warming up now, I was tired and whatever had happened to my brothers would have already happened. They'd either have started for home, or been caught by the police. Whatever, there wasn't much I could do, not right then.

'Is it a good story?' I asked.

'Oh yes,' he said, nodding his head, like my question had reminded him what it was about. 'It's a good story alright. A very good story.'

The Old Man's Story

He held the girl's eyes for a moment longer. They were the bluest he'd seen for many years, the cobalt of her irises exaggerated by the red whites, bloodshot with suppressed tears. Eventually he let them go and looked back down at the river. How much that river must have seen, he thought. How much knowledge it must have carried to the sea, how much wisdom and tragedy it must have diffused into the wide oceans of the world. He'd considered jumping into it once, balanced on the edge of London Bridge one night, the winter wind cutting into his skin. The policeman who'd talked him down had done so with one simple fact. 'You know,' he'd said, edging his way towards him, 'seven out of ten never surface. Those currents are strong. They keep them down there. We never see them again.' It had been a risk. For all the policeman had known, this was exactly what he'd wanted. But it wasn't. Although he'd come to terms with the idea of ending his life, somehow that had always involved a body, his body, being fished from the water and pulled out onto the bank. Then his remains would have finally gone home and gone into the ground there, deep into the ground. So, after the policeman told him that the river could just swallow him and leave no trace, he didn't jump after all. He'd backed away from the edge, stepped down onto the pavement, assured the young officer he would be alright and gone home. Not back home, just home.

The girl was watching him, waiting. She wanted to hear his story. That was good. He closed his eyes and tilted his face to the sun for a moment, feeling its warmth spread through his cheeks like a blush. Then, opening his eyes on the Tower again, and on the ravens strutting across its lawns, he began.

So, as I was saying, this story is about those ravens

down there. Not so much the birds themselves though; more the idea of them. I suppose you know why they're there don't you? You've heard the myth about them? No, not the fortune-telling, the other one. About what happens if they ever leave the Tower? No? Oh, well, if the ravens leave then apparently, if that ever happens, the kingdom falls. Britain will fall. Now, there's no need to look like that. I'm serious. I know that other stuff, the fortune-telling, is pretty silly, but plenty of people have credited this one with something. It's why Charles II issued a royal decree to keep six ravens at the Tower. And Winston Churchill, he certainly thought there was something in it too. Yes, Churchill. This story begins with him in a way. With Prime Minister Churchill sitting in his bunker in the war rooms, or strolling through the gardens at Chequers perhaps, thinking about those birds down there.

What I'm about to tell you happened during the Second World War. London was a frightening place back then. Especially in those early years when the Blitz was blowing up the city around us. You'd walk to work past a house one day, nod hello to the mother packing her kids off to school, gas masks bouncing round their necks – then, the very next day, you'd walk past the same house and it would be gone. You'd look for the mother and her children and you'd hope to God they'd got to the shelter in time. And then you'd walk on. Terrible. Buses blown on their sides, churches gutted, teams of men searching through piles of rubble all day long. See down there? Down the river towards the west? Well, imagine sitting here in 1940 and seeing a squadron of German bombers droning their way up the Thames like a flock of giant geese, the flak bursting all around them. That was when they were still doing daylight raids, using the river to guide them east to flatten the factories in Canning Town and Bethnal Green. Horrible, seeing them coming like that. But it was even worse when the night raids began. Then you'd only hear them, rumbling above the clouds. The searchlights made huge golden crosses over the city, then they'd swing apart again, looking for the planes up there coming to kill us. The sirens would start, then the whine of the falling ordnance; the crumple of the far explosions, the thuds and roars of the close ones. Yes, London was a frightening place to be alright back then. Very frightening.

The raids petered out after the Battle of Britain, though never completely. Russia joined the war and the whole thing went elsewhere for a while – Egypt, Italy, Greece. But towards the end, when things weren't looking too bright for the Nazis, well those raids began again. Same as before, night raids, sirens, the searchlights, but also different. They had these new rocket bombs by then you see. The V1, then the V2. You'd hear the V1 above you, day or night, a high-pitched hum above the clouds. But unlike the planes, hearing them was good. You *wanted* to hear them because that meant they were still going somewhere, still heading for somewhere else and wouldn't be dropping on you. But if you heard that humming stop, well, then you'd better run for your life. Or say goodbye to it.

This was in 1944, a few months after a friend of mine, Matthew, came to London to take up a position at the War Ministry. Now, the thing about Matthew was that he was Irish, so this wasn't even his war, let alone his ministry. Matthew O'Connell was his name. Lovely tall fellow from a small farming and fishing village on the coast south of Dublin. So what, you may ask, was he doing in London working for the British war effort? Well, you'd be surprised. Ireland was neutral in that war, but not all the Irish were. Many of their boys chose to join up and fight for the British. Brave thing to do, when you think about it, considering their fathers and grandfathers had, just a few years before, been fighting *against* the British. Ever since the Easter Rising the British had been the enemy of the Irish. So imagine looking your father in the face and telling him you were off to put on a British uniform and pick up a British gun. I happen to know that Matthew's own aunt, his father's sister, was raped by the Black and Tans, that bastard army of thugs and criminals the British brought in to keep the Irish down. Oh, I'm sorry. Forgive my language. But you understand my point, not an easy thing to do for an Irish lad, volunteer for the British army. It certainly wasn't too popular in Matthew's village, or with his family. But he went nevertheless. Why? Well, Matthew had seen what was going to happen, that's why. He'd seen the future, and not with the help of any ravens either.

He'd taken a cycle tour through Germany you see, in 1938, with his cousin who'd been teaching English there. They went all over the country that summer. They saw Germany, and they saw the Third Reich right at her heart, sucking the decency out of her like a malignant cancer. They saw it all; the marches, the parades, the uniforms, the speeches and it was as clear as day to them that war was coming, and what kind of a world it would be if the Nazis won. When a farmer in Fischbachau showed them the way to a pass through the mountains to Austria he waved them farewell with 'See you in the trenches!' shouted after them, his hands cupped around his mouth, perfectly cheerfully.

So, when the war did finally come, it only took a year or so of stalling before Matthew could no longer ignore what he had to do. Along with over a hundred thousand other Irish boys and women during the course of that war he caught a ferry to Wales, boarded a train for London and arrived here a day later, ready to volunteer for the British army.

When Matthew finished his training there was a good deal of moving between camps, more training, then retraining before he was finally posted to the new 38th Irish Infantry, part of the 78th 'Battleaxe' Division at the tail end of their campaign in Tunisia. That was where Matthew saw his first combat, in Africa. That was where he saw his first enemy prisoners and his first enemy corpse; an Afrikakorps gunner, draped over his destroyed anti-tank gun like a puppet with his strings cut. So when the 38th took part in the invasion of Sicily the next year, in July 1943, Matthew wasn't as green as he might have been. He had some idea, at least, of what lay in store for them as they waited, cramped and bobbing, in their landing crafts off the shore of Cape Passero. Not like those poor Yanks. Only action they'd ever seen was in pub brawls or whatever they'd been able to get in exchange for a couple of pairs of nylons when they'd been posted here in London.

They all did alright though, both the Irish and the Yanks. Took Messina, then went on to invade Italy too. But it was tough, very tough: 190,000 Italian soldiers on Sicily and 40,000 Germans as well. Whatever the news reports said, none of them gave up easily. Matthew was in the thick of it, and in the invasion of Italy too, but not for much of it. Piece of shrapnel the size of my fist entered his leg, here, just below the hip, and came out here, above the inside of his knee. Pretty much took out everything in between too. And that could have been it. Some serious arteries in the thigh you know? He lost a lot of blood, a lot of blood. But, thanks to one little stretcher bearer who did away with the stretcher and hauled him over his shoulder, well, Matthew made it to a medic in time. Two weeks on a hospital ship later and he was in a big country house in Kent, wheeling himself around the gardens through the falling autumn leaves, along with all the other patched, stitched, bandaged and amputated young men coming home from overseas back then.

Within a few months he was walking again, just about, but he knew he'd never be going back to the 38th, or anywhere else near the frontline. No, his war was over, in that way anyway. The army offered him honourable discharge with the full works; pension, couple of medals to show his grandchildren and a new suit to wear back home on civvy street. But Matthew didn't want to go back to civvy street and he didn't want to go back home either. Like I said, no one in his village had taken too kindly to his volunteering. It was a small place which had seen plenty of hard times. Their view was, well, close. Half of them ploughed the fields rolling down to the sea, and the other half ploughed the sea itself, hauling up bulging nets of fish from under her waves. Their physical horizons were broad – on a clear day Matthew's father reckoned he could see Wales from the top of the Wicklow hills. But their personal horizons were narrow. Matthew was pretty sure he'd be getting no hero's welcome when he returned. And he wouldn't be much use on his father's farm either, with his mangled leg. He saw himself sitting in the dark farmhouse, a drag and an embarrassment to everyone, his medals hidden in a drawer and the scar on his leg a constant reminder of what he'd done and given for the British. Doesn't sound like much fun does it? No, I'd say not. So you can understand, really, why the lad chose to stay in England instead and come here, to London.

It was Matthew's Colonel in the 38th who told him about the position at the Political Warfare Executive, and who put him up for the interview too. It was all highly irregular, what with Matthew being Irish and everything, and him having no background in the kind of thing the PWE specialised in. But his Colonel had gone to school with the interviewing officer and that, combined with Matthew's service record and an Englishman's idea of the Irish as being good liars and storytellers, ended up with Matthew being offered the position.

That was what the Political Warfare Executive did, you see. It didn't fight with conventional weapons. No, it fought with something much more powerful; an arsenal of propaganda, lies, myths and stories. The

British dabbled in this kind of thing during the First World War, but now, with the Second, well they took it to a whole new level. Nothing like a good story to get your boys fighting and their boys worried, that's what they realised. We've been living with the consequences ever since.

The PWE was established in '41, a bunch of university intellectuals and journalists. Left alone by the politicians they did a surprisingly good job. They'd plant little stories in occupied Europe and, with a bit of watering by Special Operations Executive agents, radio broadcasts, newspaper articles, with any luck those stories would grow and spread. At first, when we feared a German invasion, that's where the stories were focused, filtering tales of fearsome defences through to the ranks of the Wehrmacht. The British could set the whole Channel on fire; sharks imported from Australia to patrol the southern coast; failed invasion attempts, the bodies of horribly disfigured Germans washed up on the shores of France. That kind of thing.

Matthew was offered a clerk's position with the

Underground Rumour Mill. Now, if the PWE had been a man, the Rumour Mill wouldn't so much have been his brain as his mind; his imagination, his dark psyche. The Rumour Mill didn't bother with details of execution, leaflet drop locations, radio broadcasts. No, these people were pure, unadulterated storytellers and myth-makers; paid by the British government to lie for king and country. Working from a basement office in London and a country house in Suffolk, the Mill provided the lifeblood of the PWE – rumour and gossip capable of spreading through Europe faster than any *blitzkrieg*.

The wounds the Mill inflicted were invisible, but deep. The nightmares of a German infantryman shivering at the front; the grain of doubt taking root as a mother in Berlin listened to one of the Führer's speeches. Their orders were simple. Cook up damaging 'sibs' – from the Latin, *sibilare*, meaning to whistle or hiss – that SOE agents could whisper in the cinema queue, in the bread shop or over that quiet drink with a friend. A sib wasn't just a lie. That would have been too simple, and ineffective. No, like all the best stories sibs needed a fabric of truth through which to weave their fiction. So, information had to be gleaned first: from prisoner interrogations, from agent reports, and then fed into the Mill, who'd invent around that information before sending it back across the Channel to do its worst. When a sib turned up in conversation hundreds of miles from that first whisper, or when it was read in a captured piece of correspondence, it was ticked off as a success.

To begin with the Mill's sibs were military in nature, so they had to be approved before they went active. Stories of British 'ghost killers' stalking across Europe; fearful new super and chemical weapons, you know the kind of stuff. But as the war got nastier, so did the sibs. They became less military which meant the Mill had a free hand to get as twisted as it wanted.

The first sib across Matthew's desk was about how the fat from German army amputations was being reprocessed into soap. The inhabitants of German cities were, according to this sib, washing themselves in the limbs of their wounded soldiers. Sex,

Matthew soon realised, featured heavily in the Mill's arsenal. A necrophiliac group of SS officers, one sib reported, had assembled the 'perfect' Aryan woman from dismembered body parts of Berlin air raid victims. Pederasty, another claimed, was rife in the factories where young boys were now employed. 'Who?' the sibs asked the average German soldier, 'is doing what to your wife and your son while you risk your life for the Fatherland on the frontline?'

After two years of fighting on the frontline himself this was now Matthew's war. Processing 'sibs', copying memos and handling the expense claims of journalists who, it seemed to Matthew, often went looking for inspiration at the bottom of a bottle. He was given no part in creating the sibs himself, and no access to the information upon which they were based. He was, after all, Irish. They could only trust him so far, this was the accepted opinion. He didn't mind too much. The work was interesting enough, he had a simple room in lodgings on the Old Kent Road and a landlady who cooked a good breakfast from meagre rations, didn't ask too many questions and had her own Anderson shelter in the back garden. Not, he thought, such a bad way to see out the end of the war. Not exciting, not glamorous, not even, he sometimes felt, particularly honourable. But not bad, which, after what he'd seen in Tunisia and Italy, was fine by him. He'd done honourable and exciting with the 38th and he still lived with the consequences, limping to and from his Rumour Mill office, every day.

This, Matthew thought, was how it was going to be. He'd think about what he'd do after the war when they got there, but for now he'd resigned himself to being a pen pusher, to doing his bit for the war effort without too much, well, effort. But then one morning, out of the blue, his supervisor, Mr Seybridge, a pale, moley kind of man, dropped an order sheet onto his desk. 'There you go O'Connell,' Seybridge said. 'Something to get you out of the house.'

Matthew picked up the order sheet and glanced over it. There was a package to be collected from an address he couldn't understand. He looked up at Mr

Seybridge who'd pulled out the front of his shirt to clean his glasses, revealing a slice of plump belly, whorled with dark hair.

'Came in under "Public Morale",' he said, still cleaning his glasses and not bothering to look up at Matthew. 'Which comes under "Propaganda". Someone upstairs filed it under "Myth", which, apparently, comes under "Rumour".' He held his glasses up to the bulb hanging over Matthew's desk, then put them back on and returned Matthew's confused gaze. 'You're a farmer's lad aren't you?' he said. 'I thought this might be up your street. And anyway, we haven't got anyone else we can spare right now.' He spread a sudden smile across his face. 'So, enjoy!'

With that Seybridge turned and walked away, calling over his shoulder, 'Sally's got your tickets. You leave in the morning.'

Matthew looked back down at the order sheet. A single typed line at the top said it had been issued by the office of the Prime Minister. At the bottom of the page, under the address he couldn't understand, was an inventory of the package contents.

WHITE RAVENS

```
6 x Raven chicks
```

The pick-up address was Welsh, that's why he hadn't
been able to understand it. From the length of the
names and the number of consonants it looked as
if the place was deep into the country. He flipped
the page to look at the Photostat stapled behind. It
was a piece of standard government copy like many
he'd seen before, pulled from a file somewhere
within the bureaucratic labyrinth of Whitehall. He
read the title.

```
        The Tower Ravens
Six ravens have been kept at the Tower of
London by Royal decree since Charles II was
asked to remove the birds at the request
of the Astronomer Royal (Flamsteed, John)
because they were 'disturbing his examina-
tions of the heavens'. The King - informed of
the myth that if the ravens leave the Tower,
the Tower of London, the White Tower, the
monarchy and the kingdom of Britain would
fall - refused Flamsteed's request and issued
a Royal decree for a full complement of six
```

```
ravens to be kept at the Tower at all times.
The Royal observatory was moved to Greenwich.
```

A single handwritten note at the bottom of the Photostat completed the order sheet. 'One surviving Raven. Re-stock tower with new chicks from above address. Escorted collection and delivery required. By order of the PM.' And that was it: one typed line, the address, the inventory, a bit of folklore history and this handwritten note. Matthew saw the logic behind it; Churchill couldn't allow the Tower to go ravenless, not at such a crucial point in the war. No doubt the Nazis had their own Rumour Mill over there and it was the kind of thing they'd enjoy making a meal of. A mythical portent of Britain's inevitable defeat. Nothing but superstition, but God knows, hadn't they made use of such stuff themselves? But he still didn't understand. Why an escorted collection? Couldn't they just send for the birds? Picking the order sheet off his desk, he went to find Seybridge.

'Yes?' Seybridge already sounded bored, as if he

knew exactly who was going to walk through his door. 'What is it O'Connell?'

'This order sheet sir,' Matthew said as he entered. 'I don't understand. I mean, seems like a lot of trouble doesn't it? Just for some birds?'

Seybridge sat back heavily in his chair. 'Does it now?'

'Well, yes sir, it does. Couldn't they just send for them?'

Seybridge sighed. He looked to the side of his office, as if hoping to discover a window to stare out of wisely. There was none, so he looked at the exposed pipes running under the ceiling instead.

'Have you taken a look in butchers' windows recently O'Connell?'

'Sorry sir?'

'Butchers. Have you looked in their windows recently?' he said, looking back at Matthew over his glasses. 'They're selling crows now. And ravens. Anything with a bit of meat on it. You're going to escort those birds back to the Tower to stop some bugger eating them. That's why.'

'Oh,' Matthew said, 'I see, yes sir.'

'That order found its way to us,' Seybridge continued, sitting forward to his desk. 'So we'll take care of it. Look, I know it's an odd one but I thought you wouldn't mind actually.' He looked almost hurt, as if he'd given Matthew a gift, not an order, and now here he was ungratefully returning it to him. 'I thought you might even appreciate a trip out of the city, get back to nature and all that.'

'Right,' Matthew said, unsure what to make of Seybridge's sudden paternal concern.

Then, just as suddenly, it was gone. 'Is that all?' Seybridge asked, lowering his eyes to the papers layering his desk.

'Yes sir,' Matthew replied. 'That's all.'

He turned for the door. As he opened it Seybridge spoke again. 'Try to enjoy it O'Connell,' he said. 'That's my advice. Some time away from this place. It'll do you good.'

'Yes,' Matthew said, 'thank you sir.'

Closing the door behind him Matthew walked away from Seybridge's office down the long subterranean corridor back to his own desk, wondering as he went what exactly one should pack for a trip to collect some ravens from Wales.

The order hadn't said anything about a horse. If it had he might have packed differently. This is what Matthew thought when he saw the boy holding the mud-spattered grey gelding outside the one-track station. The boy, no more than ten years old, held the horse in one hand and clutched a torn piece of cardboard to his chest with the other. 'O'Connell' was scrawled across it in what looked like charcoal. There was another pony, a long-maned little skewbald tethered behind the gelding.

Matthew looked around the station, abandoned on the bare hill. The train he'd arrived on was already backing away down the track, trailing heavy gobs of steam. His fellow passengers were also leaving, walking towards the scrappy town in the valley below. Farmers back from market, a couple of office clerks, a woman with a gaggle of evacuee kids, their cockney accents exotic against the terraced houses backed by miles and miles of moorland and hills. Matthew looked back at the boy. 'Are you here for me?' he asked him.

The boy looked down at the piece of cardboard, as

if maybe Matthew hadn't seen it. 'Yer'im?' he asked. He had a strong accent which ran the two words into one. 'Yes,' Matthew said. 'That's me. I was expecting Constable Jones? He was meant to take me to, to...' he fumbled in his pocket for the name of the farm which he still couldn't pronounce.

''E couldn' come,' the boy said, cutting Matthew's search short. ''E said as 'e wouldn' be wastin' any petrol on some Londoner. 'E said as not with the rationin'. 'E said as yer can have an 'orse 'stead, 'cos an 'orse is good enough for every one else, so it's as good enough for yew.'

The boy paused, apparently as surprised as Matthew by his own burst of eloquence. ''E said as I was t' show yer up t' Llewellyn's,' he added, just in case Matthew hadn't understood. Which he hadn't. Not every word anyway, although he'd managed to grasp what they meant. He'd be riding to the farm with this boy. Over eight miles at least, from what he remembered from the map he'd studied at the PWE. A lonely square marking the farm, marooned in a stream of tight contours, surrounded by green and brown and not another little square for miles. It was already late in the afternoon. He'd had to take three trains just to get this far already. He saw no other choice but to agree.

'Right,' he said. 'I see. Well, we'd best get going then hadn't we?' He tried a smile on the boy, hoping to crack his dour seriousness. The boy handed him the gelding's reins in reply, as serious as ever, took his case from him, then went to the little skewbald behind.

'I'm Matthew,' Matthew said over the horse's back. Surely they should at least be introduced before they rode into the hills together? The boy, still strapping Matthew's case to the side of the skewbald, turned and nodded again. 'I know,' he said hitching himself up onto the pony and, with a yank at its bit, kicking it on up a track leading from the station up into the hills.

The track was steep and soon left the scattered vestiges of the little town behind it; the sheds backing onto the station, a single dark cottage with a garden making a brave attempt on the bare moorland slope. As the track became a path, even narrower and strewn with loose stones, they passed a lonely farm with a couple of cattle slow-chewing on a pile of hay. The blonde crop seemed to glow in the gathering evening, still warm with the summer day it was cut. Matthew looked behind him as they climbed and saw the town he'd arrived in had literally been at the end of the line. The railway tracks, cutting smoothly up from the valley below, stopped abruptly beneath the roof of the station. Beyond that roof the town was already winking with lights, lamps and candles lighting up in its windows, only to go out again behind the thick material of the blackout curtains.

All day Matthew's journey had been a diminishing one: from the vaulted hall of Paddington station, its crowds knotted with soldiers and gaggles of sailors laden with guns, rucksacks, helmets and all the paraphernalia of war. Then, as his train had shunted through the suburbs out of the city, those crowds had shrunk to the six people of his carriage compartment. A tearful evacuee boy, an American sergeant who already looked too old to be joining a fight anywhere, a harried-looking clerk with his family and a nervous-looking Wren who bit her nails all the way to Swindon. All bore the wearied faces of war. Maybe Seybridge was right, Matthew had thought, perhaps it really would do him some good to get out of the city for a day or two.

As the train rolled west Matthew and the sergeant swapped stories from the Italian campaign. The sergeant had got there more or less as Matthew had left, a few days after the little stretcher bearer had shouldered him down to the field hospital. He'd fought right through the country and now, he said in a thick southern accent, 'I guess we'll be going over there again, soon enough.' He was also on his way to Wales, to join thousands of other GIs training there. He didn't say what they were training for and Matthew didn't ask. Everyone knew something big was coming and that men like this sergeant would be in the frontline. For the last few miles into Cardiff he'd sat very still opposite Matthew, looking through his own reflection at the passing countryside and occasionally down at a tattered photograph he'd pull from his pocket. Matthew guessed it held the face of either a girl, or those of a wife and child. Whichever, both were far away from him, thousands of miles across the sea from this train edging towards Wales.

Matthew detrained at Cardiff, caught another, smaller train to a smaller, higher town, and then an even smaller train again to this smallest, highest town yet. And now here he was, at the end of his day, his travels diminished to just him and this silent boy, riding together higher into the darkening mountains.

The grey gelding was broad-backed and rocked comfortably beneath Matthew. According to the boy it had no name, so Matthew privately christened the horse Mullie, after a Scottish corporal he'd met at the hospital in Kent. Mullie's hair had turned the same colour as this gelding's coat, shockingly white, after he'd been blown out of his tank somewhere in the Western desert. Corporal Mullie had been left grumpily hobbling round on one leg. His equine namesake, in contrast, was remarkably sure-footed and good natured, given every now and then to shaking his head with sudden comforting snorts through his nostrils. As the evening got darker Matthew felt a growing affection for Mullie, for the blind dutifulness with which he carried him, a complete stranger, upon his back up into the hills. He wished he could have said the same about the boy, but it wouldn't have been true. Matthew had made several attempts at conversation, but each to no avail. The boy knew what he had to do, just as dutifully as Mullie, and he obviously wasn't going to do much else. So Matthew was thankful when, a couple of hours after they'd left the station, the boy pulled up his skewbald and pointed a finger into the distance. 'Tha's it,' he said.

Matthew strained his eyes in the direction the boy pointed. There was still just enough light in the spring evening for him to make out a dwelling of some kind on the horizon. And a barn maybe, and perhaps even a walled pen for animals. The sound of stones dislodging from the path behind him made Matthew turn around. The boy was already yanking at the skewbald's bit and jabbing at it with his heels, pushing it on down the path, handing Matthew his case as he passed.

Matthew watched as the rounded rump of the skewbald faded into the darkness until there was just the sound of its hooves picking its way carefully down the mountain. The boy had brought him within sight of the farm and that, obviously, had been enough for him. His job done he'd left without another word or gesture. 'Well Mullie,' Matthew found himself saying aloud, 'I suppose it's just us now.' Clutching his case to his chest he tapped the horse's sides and Mullie, shifting his weight slowly, began making his way up the path just as carefully as the little skewbald had picked its way down.

As Matthew neared the farmhouse the mountain rose higher behind it, its towering bulk edging into the sky to slip the farm further under the horizon until Matthew could no longer make out its shape against the slope. No light came from the farm. He couldn't tell if the windows were thoroughly blacked out, or if there were just no lights burning behind them in the first place. Unless someone had pointed the farm out, you could have walked right past at night and never have known it was there.

When he reached the threshold Matthew dismounted and tied Mullie beside a water trough laid into a low wall surrounding the house. For a moment he did nothing else. The farm was impossibly still and he felt as if any movement would have been an imposition in some way, a blasphemous act upon the silent buildings. There was no sign of any animals, no trees to move or make a sound in the wind and no sign of human activity at all.

As he stood there wondering what to do the first light of the rising moon diffused along the mountain's edge, as if someone had put a match to a trail of magnesium. By this faint light the farm began to reveal itself. Matthew made out stone slates layered over the roof; cracked paving stones leading to a heavy front door set in a foreshortened porch; the sentry of a milk urn, standing to attention beside the coal scullery.

Until now Mullie too, it seemed, had been struck

still by the impassive farmhouse. But now, with that first light, he dropped his head to the trough and began to drink. The brightening moonlight lit the steam rising along his neck, and rippled through the trough like a sudden shoal of fish as his muzzle broke the water's surface.

Emboldened by the light, and by the sound of Mullie drinking, Matthew approached the farm's front door. There was no knocker so he rapped loudly with his knuckles, three times. The raps died instantly in the thick wood. No echo, no resonance. Matthew wouldn't have been surprised if they weren't heard, even by someone standing right on the other side. Stepping around the porch, he tried to look through a lower window but all he saw was the ghost of his own reflection, looming in the pane before being obscured by his own breath against the glass. Moving backwards from the house, he looked it over, as if he were a burglar sizing it up for a way in. Because he did have to get in, there was no doubt about that. The night was turning cold and he wasn't going to just turn around and ride back into the town, not after coming all this way. Not with an order from the Prime Minister's office in his pocket.

Taking a deep breath, Matthew called out to the tomb-like farmhouse, 'Hello? Hello?' He strained to listen for a response. When it came, it did so not in the form of a voice, but a memory. A sudden, distinct sound that Matthew had heard many times before, and which he recognised immediately. A scraping of metal, the faint whirr of heavy motion, and then the sparking of metal again, slid along moving stone. Matthew had heard that sound all through his childhood, whenever the tinkers came to his father's yard. There it was again – a whirring and sparking. He could see the sandstone wheel in his mind, and then the steel again, thinning against that turning wheel, spitting sparks from its edge. That wheel wasn't turning on its own. Someone's hand was winding its handle. Someone was sharpening a blade. But not a knife. Whatever blade this was, it was much heavier and longer than a knife.

Following the sound, Matthew went around the

side of the farmhouse, stumbling over the rutted ground, one hand held before him to ward off ambushes by unseen objects in the dark. Reaching the side of the house he used its end wall to guide him, running his palm across its rough stones as he walked, the intermittent hush and scrape of the sharpening blade getting louder all the time. Rounding the far corner he saw the sloping roof of a lean-to, slanted against the back of the farm. The building, a crude addition to the main farmhouse, was cracked with light from within, shining from the edges of an ill-fitting door, through a space between the top of the wall and the roof beam, through a crooked slit window and, in a couple of places, even between the stones from which it was built.

The sharpening sound was coming from inside this lean-to. Matthew stood there in the dark, listening to the steel angling to the wheel, to the delicate friction of its edge against the stone. Having found the source, he wasn't sure what to do next, and he was still considering his options when the sound of the turning wheel began to slow, then stopped.

Before he could move, the crack of light at one side of the door started to widen, laying down a broad-ening path of yellow lamplight over the grass. The light captured Matthew in its lengthening beam, and then, just as suddenly, went out again, as the huge bulk of a man appeared at the door.

At first sight Matthew thought the figure was headless. A massive body holding a large axe, the blade of which caught the lamplight shining from behind. But then the man stepped through the door and, straightening to his full height, revealed, to Matthew's great relief, a head of wild, unruly hair. That relief soon turned to astonishment. Now he was no longer bending to get through the door, Matthew saw that the man stood as tall as the lean-to itself, the roof of which was at least seven foot from the ground.

For a few seconds the two of them stood there like that, facing each other in the darkness. Matthew couldn't stop looking at the axe in the man's hand. Combined with the night's strange ride, the looming mountains all around him and the silent, dark farmhouse, it stopped his tongue in his mouth. So it was only when Ben Llewellyn stepped away from the door, allowing the lamplight to fall across Matthew again, that he saw his visitor standing there, dumbstruck in the middle of the dark field behind his house.

'Oh!' Ben said, genuinely surprised. 'Hello there. Is that you Mr O'Connell?'

His voice was as deep as he was tall; a rich accent undulating with the timbre of the mountains in which he lived. 'How long you been there? Not too long I hope?'

Matthew cleared his throat, aware how ridiculous he must look, clutching his city case in the darkness. 'Oh, no. Just arrived actually.' He pointed vaguely towards Mullie, tethered unseen on the other side of the house.

'Have you now? Well, I'm glad to hear that,' Ben said, striding towards him with his hand extended. '*Croeso*, Mr O'Connell, welcome.'

'Matthew is fine.'

'Ben. Ben Llewellyn. Pleased to meet you

Matthew.' The palm of Ben's hand enveloped Matthew's easily, its skin as rough as the bark of a hundred-year-old oak.

'I was jus' goin' to cut some wood for your fire, but let's leave tha' for now shall we? Come on, let's get you inside is it? Here, let me take that.' Ben took Matthew's case from him as if it were empty. 'Must be hungry,' he continued as he led the way to the farm's back door.

'Er, yes,' Matthew replied. 'I'd say so.'

'Is tha' an Irish accent?' Ben said over his shoulder as he searched on a shelf inside the door.

'Yes, it is.'

'Lovely country,' Ben said, striking a match and putting it to the wick of a candle. 'Never been there myself, but tha's what I'm told anyway. Now, let's see wha' Bran's left for you.'

Matthew followed his host down a narrow white-washed corridor, the candle's illumination reaching just far enough for him to make out Ben's wild hair brushing the ceiling as he walked.

'*Duw*, Jones, tha' old bastard. Fancy havin' you come up by the track.' Ben shook his head as he ladled out a bowl of soup, still smiling at what Matthew had told him. ''E could have brought you up in his car, easy,' he continued, placing the bowl in front of Matthew. 'Jus' making a point I'll bet. Got a chip on hisself see? 'Bout English – Londoners 'specially. Might 'ave been different had he known you was Irish.'

'Right,' Matthew said, blowing across a spoonful of the soup. 'Though you'd think the name would have given him a clue.'

'Ha, well, yes.' Ben laughed, leaning against the range beside the fire, tipping his head forward to fit himself under the ceiling. 'But Jones, well, not the brightest spark, know what I'm sayin'?'

'So there's a lane comes here?' Matthew asked, feeling the two hours of his night's ride against the hard seat of his chair.

'Course there is mun!' Ben laughed again. 'Think we come an' go on tha' track? It's over the other side of the hill, so the track's quicker on a 'orse, but in a cart or a car, down t' town in under an hour you are.'

'I see,' Matthew said.

'Well, least you got to see a bit of the place isn't it?' Ben said, pushing himself away from the range. 'On the way up I mean.' He spoke through a simultaneous smile and frown, as if he was perpetually bemused at the ridiculousness of the world. Maybe, Matthew thought, it was an attitude that had grown as he'd grown himself; as he'd increasingly discovered himself outsized in proportion to everything else. Watching him now, as he bent to prod the fire and take the pot of soup over to the kitchen counter, Matthew saw he really was a giant of a man. His neck was as thick as Matthew's thigh, while his back, when he turned away, was as broad as two normal men's together. Now he had his sleeves rolled up, Matthew saw his forearms were as thick and knotted as the largest ropes the navy had used in Sicily. Wherever he moved within the farmhouse it seemed to shrink about him; walls tightened, ceilings lowered, tables and chairs became doll's-house furniture. Matthew, in proportion with these same tables and chairs, felt like a child in his presence.

'Well,' Ben said, through a sigh, 'I'd better see to this 'orse Jones borrowed you hadn't I?'

Shouldering on a jacket he bowed into the porch, closing the door behind him. Matthew heard the outer door close, then Ben's deep voice, addressing Mullie, '*Helo... sut wyt ti heno, te?*' then Mullie's snort in reply, thick and grateful, as if he knew Ben of old.

As Matthew finished his soup, mopping up the bowl with a chunk of bread like he hadn't tasted in years, he looked about the kitchen. The place wasn't dissimilar to his father's farm in Ireland, shaped and ordered by the same daily routine of farming and cooking, of feeding and being fed. Boots in the corner, sheep shears on the dresser, cans, pumps and tubes of ointments and sprays stacked up on a shelf by the door. As well as this detritus of work the room also revealed some of the life lived there too. A glass casement with a diorama of a fox, frozen in the moment after it had killed a goose, stood against one wall. The animal's head was up, ears pricked, as if it had just been disturbed. Its jaws were full of white feathers tipped with blood at their quills and its glass eyes stared intently over its shoulder, its body tensed above the body of the goose, lying limp in the ferns and grass under him. Beside this casement were some bookshelves. Matthew scanned the spines but all the titles were in Welsh. On the other side of the room a Welsh dresser was hung with crockery, dented tankards and the wooden links of a Welsh love spoon. On its surface, among the shears and scraps of paper and pamphlets, were a few framed photographs. A young man in uniform, from this war, not the First. Another, much older photo, of a couple standing outside the farmhouse with a sheep dog, its paw faithfully placed on his master's thigh as man and wife stared sternly towards the camera. There was one of Ben too, beaming his perplexed smile, bending to hold a magnificent ram, a large rosette blossoming on one of its horns. At the very top of the dresser, glowing faintly in the gloom, was a bird's skull, its long beak tapering away from the hollow shell of its head.

Ben had mentioned a woman, Bran, but he hadn't

said whether she was a wife or a daughter. Pushing back his chair Matthew stood to have a closer look around the room, hoping to find some feminine trace to give him a clue. He was at the dresser, looking over the photos again when he heard the kitchen door opening.

'There you go,' Ben said as he entered. 'Happy enough now alright.'

'Thank you,' Matthew said, going back to the table to take his bowl to the sink.

'Oh, leave that, leave that,' Ben said, taking the bowl from him and turning to run it under the tap. For some reason Matthew felt guilty, as if he'd been caught snooping. 'You know you're too early don't you?'

'I'm sorry?'

Ben turned to face him. 'Too early. For the birds. They've sent you too early. They've only jus' hatched. Take 'em now and they'll die on you.'

'Oh,' Matthew said. 'Really?'

Ben saw Matthew glance at his overnight case. 'Tha' a problem you reckon?'

'Um, no,' Matthew said. 'No. But, well, how long do you think it'll be? Before I can take them?'

Ben raised his eyebrows and shrugged off his jacket to hang it on a rack behind the kitchen door. 'You in a hurry to get back?' he said, speaking into the wad of coats and overalls.

'Well, I'm expected back soon. I've got a ticket for the day after tomorrow.'

Ben turned to face him again, looking down seriously from his great height. 'We're all expected somewhere sometime,' he said. 'But is there somethin' waitin' for you? Or someone?'

Matthew thought of the single room in his lodgings on the Old Kent Road, of the bombed houses like missing teeth in the smile of the crescent. He thought of his desk at the PWE, the stack of memos piling up in the in-tray, of Mr Seybridge cleaning his glasses on his shirt. 'No,' he said. 'Not really.'

'Well, there you go then,' Ben said, apparently energised by Matthew's response. Striding across the room he plucked Matthew's case off the floor and swung open a door onto a staircase spiralling steeply up to the floor above. 'I'll show you yer room,' Ben said, picking up a lamp in his other hand and somehow managing to fold himself into the staircase. Matthew followed him, still unclear as to how long he'd be staying in this room to which Ben was showing him.

Ben was saying goodnight, having made sure Matthew had everything he needed, when he paused at the door. 'I hope you don't mind me asking, Mr O'Connell,' he said through one of his bemused smiles. 'But you do know why you've come here for those birds don't you?'

'Yes,' Matthew said as he opened his case on the bed. 'The Tower of London isn't it? Ravens leave, Tower and kingdom falls. All that…' he tailed off, his sentence losing energy under the furrows of Ben's frown.

'Yes,' Ben said slowly, taking a step back into the room. 'All that indeed. But do you know why all that?'

Matthew laughed awkwardly, wishing Ben hadn't thrown his words back at him in that way. It had been a very long day and he could do without an interrogation right now. 'No,' he said, smiling, though with less conviction now. 'I suppose I don't. Six raven chicks, from here to there. That's all I know really.'

Ben nodded. 'Wait here a minute will you Mr O'Connell?'

'Matthew, please.' But Ben had already left the room. Matthew followed the sound of his heavy steps, which made the whole house creak like a ship in storm, down the corridor, down the stone stairs and across the kitchen in three clean strides. There was a pause before the same pattern was reversed to bring Ben and his lamp back to Matthew's door. He was holding a book this time, bound in dark leather with gold lettering on its spine.

'The Second Branch,' Ben said, holding out the book.

'Sorry?'

'The Second Branch,' he said again, nudging the book further towards him. '"Branwen Daughter of Llyr". You should read it. Don't worry, this one's in English.'

Matthew took the book and, opening it, tried to pronounce the word on its title page. 'The Mab... Mabi... Mabn...'

'The *Mabinogion*,' Ben said. 'Four branches of ancient myths. You should read the second, might shed some light on yer little journey tonight.'

'Right,' Matthew said.

Ben seemed unconvinced. 'It's important we know why we go where we do Mr O'Connell,' he said. 'These stories are still with us for a reason you know.'

Matthew flipped a page and saw a name inscribed along the dotted line of a faded purple stamp. The book had been a school prize, presented to... again he tried to pronounce the letters before him, and again Ben had to help him out.

'Bendigeidfran Llewellyn,' he said. 'That's me. You can see why I go by Ben.'

'Yes, quite a name you got there,' Matthew said.

'Means "magnificent crow" in English, or... ' Ben leant forwards for effect, "raven".'

'And Branwen?' Matthew said pointing at the name in the title on the contents page. 'Is that the full name of your…?' He left the question hanging, hoping Ben would finish for him again. He didn't. He just nodded, smiling his old bemused smile.

'Yes, that's right. Branwen. Means "white crow" or "white raven". So, Mr O'Connell,' Ben continued, turning into the corridor. 'As you can see, you've come t' the right place for those birds.'

With that Ben left him. Matthew watched his huge figure, silhouetted by the light of his lamp, retreat down the corridor away from his room, his hair brushing along the ceiling once more, his voice trailing deeply behind him. 'Oh yes, you've come to the right place alright.'

It was late the next morning when Matthew surfaced from the depths of his night's sleep. The farmhouse, so quiet when he'd arrived, was now at the centre of a mountain orchestra of wind, bleating lambs and birdsong. As Matthew fully crossed into waking, he could also make out, coming from somewhere in the house underneath him, the strains of a woman's voice, singing.

Opening his eyes he sat up in bed to look around the bedroom. It was simple and neat, washed through with spring sunshine from the one small window. The previous day's journey felt unreal in the bold clarity of this light. Had he really ridden up that track with the boy? Had he really seen Ben Llewellyn, a giant of a man, unfold from the lean-to shed, an axe dangling from his arm? Yes, the ache along the inside of his thighs confirmed the ride and there, on the bedside table, was the book Ben had given him last night, unopened, the gold lettering of its title catching a tight beam of light shining through a crack in the curtains.

When Matthew drew back those curtains the full extent of his isolation was revealed to him, in all its drama. A long sweep of cleanly sculpted mountains curved away from the farm on either side, like two huge waves rushing together, a maelstrom stilled just moments before collision. Between these mountains, smaller hills and hummocks of moorland echoed each other into the distance, melting into a hazy horizon. There was nothing else. Some strewn patches of scree, grey against the mountain slopes, some protruding rocks, finely carved by thousands of years of weather and ice, the tail end of the track he'd ridden up the previous night and a few high clouds in the blue sky. Matthew couldn't remember when he'd been able to see so far. From the deck of the ship that took him to Sicily, certainly. But on land? Probably when his father, after listening to his reasons for volunteering, had walked him to the summit of one of the Wicklow hills and shown him his country stretched before him, as if that would have been enough to convince him to stay. Behind them, where his father hadn't wanted to look that day, had been the sea, and beyond it a faint smudge on the horizon, that his father had once told him was the mountains of Wales.

As he washed and dressed Matthew heard the woman's voice again, rising from below. It was only when he was in the corridor, however, walking towards the stairs, that he properly heard her song. Halfway down the stairs he stopped to listen more closely. He could hear the words clearly now, but he couldn't understand any of them. The song, like the titles of the books along the bookcase, was in Welsh. A slow, plaintive tune that doubled back and worked itself round to a particularly haunting refrain. It was lovely and, Matthew thought, as he listened to it through the closed door, all the more so because he couldn't follow its meaning. The story of the song was lost on him, but that was all that was lost; just the tale. The music itself, and the woman's voice, he understood these clearly. It was as if it was a song he'd always known, but only just discovered on hearing it sung through a door in a house he'd yet to see in daylight, by a woman he'd never met.

Stirring himself, Matthew eventually carried on down the stairs and opened the door at the bottom. As soon as the latch clicked, the song stopped. Matthew stepped into the room, immediately sorry he'd disturbed the singer whose voice had so given the song life.

'Well, someone slept well, didn' they?'

She was standing beside the table, a dishcloth draped over one shoulder, holding a knife in one hand, her other resting on the back of a chair. A small vase of primroses stood at the centre of the table where she was laying a single place before the same chair Matthew had sat in the previous night. Her dark hair was long enough to be bundled in a loose knot at the back of her head. She wore an off-white apron over a simple short-sleeved dress. Her features were supple and fine as if the edges of her face, the line of her nose, her cheekbones, her jaw, had been winnowed by the same millennia of winds and rains that had carved the rocks he'd seen from his window. Her skin was pale, and her eyes bluer than Matthew knew eyes could be. She was beautiful and on seeing her, the resonance of her song and her voice still hanging in the air, Matthew fell immediately and deeply in love. It was as if he'd opened that door into a different world, not a different room. With one step into it the colour and taste of his life had changed, shot through as it now was from this moment on, and as it always would be, so powerfully with her.

'I made you some breakfast,' she said, laying the knife in place. 'Though lord knows, it's more like yer lunch now.' Bending down at the range she covered her hand with the dishcloth and took out a plate of bacon from the warming shelf. The smell of it spread through the kitchen. When was the last time he'd smelt bacon like that? Never since he'd left home, that was for sure. Placing the plate on the table she pulled back the chair and, raising her eyebrows, invited him to sit down.

'Thank you,' he said, looking around the room for a clock. There wasn't one and his own watch lay beside his bed upstairs. 'What time is it?'

She was at the counter, her back to him, slicing some eggs she'd boiled. 'Around eleven I'd say,' she said, peering out of the window. 'Or half-past.'

Was that really the best he could do? The first time he addresses her and he chooses a question you'd ask any stranger in the street. As she tipped the slices of egg onto his plate he tried again.

'I'm Matthew.'

'I know who you are,' she said, turning back to the

counter. 'Ben told me.'

He waited for her to introduce herself, but she carried on preparing some potatoes as if he wasn't there. She'd begun to hum the song again.

'I hope I didn't wake you last night, coming in so late.'

'Wake me? *Duw*, I wouldn' worry about that *bach*,' she said without turning round. 'I wasn' even here.'

She was making him feel foolish, like a little boy.

'Where were you?'

The question sounded blunt and clumsy on his ear.

'Down at the exchange.'

'The exchange?'

''Mergency telephone exchange. Got t' do yer bit haven' you? Though since they stopped bombing there hasn' been much emergency about it.'

Turning around she leant back against the counter, wiping her hands on her apron. When he looked up she was smiling, as if she'd stopped playing with him now. 'I do the late shift. Once a week.'

'Right, I see. Yes.'

For a moment neither of them spoke. The sun lit swirling motes of dust in a broad beam that fell through the kitchen. The bleats of lambs and bird-song filtered through to them. Matthew felt an urgent pressure to speak, to say something, anything.

'Lovely flowers,' he said at last, nodding at the primroses on the table.

She smiled again, acknowledging his awkwardness. Pulling out a chair she sat down beside him 'So,' she said leaning forward and placing her elbows carefully on the table. 'You've come for the birds?'

'Yes,' Matthew said, glad to be answering a question rather than asking one. 'That's right.'

Suddenly, she was laughing. A bright, full laugh, and shaking her head as if in disbelief, loosening the dark knot of her hair, a few strands falling free. And then, because she was, he was laughing too, though at what or why he didn't know.

'What is it?' he asked her.

'Oh,' she said, speaking through a deep breath. 'Nothin' really. It's jus' well, ridiculous isn't it? I mean Ben used to get such a tellin' off for going' up there an' stealin' eggs an' such. He even had a pet one once. A raven! You can imaging the trouble tha' caused when Mam found out.' She shook her head again. 'An' now he's stealing them for bloody Churchill!' she said, dissolving into another fit of laughter.

This time Matthew didn't join in and when she turned to him something in his expression must have betrayed the question burning in him. She stopped laughing. 'Ben's my brother,' she said slowly, as if speaking to a child. 'My older brother.'

'Right,' Matthew said. 'Of course. I wasn't sure...'

Shaking her head at him again she cleared away his plate and brought the kettle from the range to pour him a mug of tea. 'So, do you think there's anything in it?' she said, sitting again.

'In what?'

'The story. 'Bout the ravens an' the Tower.'

Matthew shifted in his chair. 'Well,' he said, cupping his hands around the tea. 'These stories, they're still with us for a reason aren't they?' She didn't look convinced.

'Are they?' she said sitting back in her chair and

folding her arms across her chest.

'Churchill obviously thinks so,' he said. 'Public morale and all that.'

'An' tha's what you do then is it? Fix up our morale?'

'Something like that I suppose,' he said. 'I work in propaganda.'

'Ah' she said, nodding. 'More stories.'

'Yes,' he admitted. 'More stories.'

This felt better; talking like equals. She no longer seemed to be merely tolerating him among her daily chores. 'How long do you think it'll be,' he asked her. 'Before I can take them?'

'Well, let's see,' she said, leaning forward again. 'They've jus' hatched, so it'll be three weeks before they leave the nest. You wouldn' want to take them then though, they'd be too strong already. No, so say, 'bout two weeks? That should be 'bout right.'

'Two weeks?' he said nodding slowly. 'I see.'

A slow bloom of elation opened in his chest. He took a drink of the tea, pouring the liquid's warmth over that rare flower and sat back in his chair, trying not to reveal the sudden lightness he felt inside.

'Somethin' like tha' anyway,' she continued, standing again. 'Ben'll know better.' She looked out of the window again. 'He's on the hill. I should go an' see if he wants help. You got everythin' you need?'

'Yes,' Matthew said standing too. 'Yes, I have. Thank you.'

As she put on her coat, taking it off the same rack Ben had hung his on the night before, she spoke to him again. 'What happened to yer leg?'

'My leg?' Matthew said, caught unawares by the question.

'You were limpin' when you came down jus' now. You hurt it?'

Matthew instinctively reached for the scar on his thigh. 'I was wounded,' he said. 'In Italy. A while ago now.'

'Oh,' she said, glancing at the photograph of the young man in uniform on the dresser. 'I'm sorry.'

It was impossible for Matthew not to react to that glance. 'Is he away?' he asked, hoping to God the poor man was still alive.

'Evan? Yes, he is. Been gone for over a year now.'

'Your husband?' Matthew surprised himself with the boldness of his question, but he had to know.

'No,' she said, giving him a gentle smile. 'Evan's my younger brother. Tha's his room yer sleepin' in. Farm wasn' big enough to keep him out the fightin'.' She went over to the dresser and picked up the photograph. 'We haven' heard a thing for months.'

'Do you know where he is?'

She sighed heavily, putting the photograph back. 'Last letter we got was from India. We think 'e's in Burma now, far as we know.'

Burma. None of the fronts were easy in this war Matthew knew but Burma... Matthew looked around the farmhouse, Evan's home, and tried to imagine the boy from here out there in the jungle, the heat, the flies, caught up in all that silent terror and sudden killing. He hoped for her sake he'd come back one day and that, when he did, his sister would still know him as her brother.

'I'm sure he's fine,' Matthew said, trying to sound as reassuring as possible.

'Yes,' she said, trying another smile but failing this time. 'I'm sure he is.' She looked back at the photograph, and this time held the stare of the young man within its frame. When she finally broke away Matthew saw her eyes had filmed with tears.

'Well,' she said. 'Can't stand 'ere talkin' all day. I'll be back to make up supper. If you want anythin' 'fore then there's bread an' jam in the larder there.' She pointed at a large walk-in cupboard at the end of the kitchen. 'By the way,' she added as she opened the door. 'I'm Branwen.' And with that she was gone.

As soon as she'd closed the door behind her Matthew went straight to the window to catch a glimpse of her walking around the corner of the farmhouse. Realising she must be going up to the lower slopes behind the house, he went back across the kitchen to the spiral stairway and climbed it as fast as his leg would let him. He knew he was acting like the foolish boy she'd made him feel earlier, but he didn't care. He had to see her again; it was as simple as that. Following the narrow corridor away from his bedroom he found a small window and, looking out of it, caught one more glimpse of her walking up and over the rise behind the house, her arms raised as she tied the knot of her loosened hair.

Matthew had woken up that morning asking himself how long before he'd be leaving the farmhouse. Standing at that small window, just an hour later, watching Branwen walk away up the hill, he felt strong with resolve. Not because he'd found the answer to his question but, as with all the crucial hinges in our lives, because the question itself had changed. It was no longer about when he could leave, but how he could leave with her? When could he take her away with him? Away from this farm, this isolated mountain, and into a new life in which they'd share the future together?

'Would you like a piece?'

The old man held out the half-finished slab of chocolate he'd brought with him, unfolding the silver wrapping to reveal the scored dark squares inside.

'What?'

'A piece. Of chocolate. Would you like one? I know I shouldn't, this early in the day. But, well, sweet tooth I suppose.'

The girl didn't reply, just looked at the offered chocolate like it was a trick. Eventually, with exaggerated caution, she took the slab from him and broke off a couple of squares. Tourists were beginning to trickle into the Tower now. The first air-conditioned coaches were lining up down from the bridge to disgorge their Germans, their Japanese and their value-weekend trippers from towns in the north, south and west. All come to gawp at the jewels, to hear about Anne Boleyn's restless ghost wandering the grounds and, of course, to see the ravens.

'Well?' the girl said from beside him. He sucked luxuriously on the diminishing chocolate in his mouth. Thank God he still had his own teeth.

'Well?' he asked her back.

'Are you goin' carry on or what? With the story.'

'Oh the story!' he said arching his eyebrows. 'Do you have time?'

She looked past him at a crocodile line of tourists following their guide's furled umbrella towards the main gate. He should be careful. He could still lose her and he couldn't risk that, not now.

'Yes,' she finally said, still looking away. 'I've got time.'

'Oh, good. Well now, where was I?'

She looked back at him, a hardness in her blue eyes. She knew he was playing with her now. 'Your friend was gettin' all worked up over this girl he'd just met,' she said, handing him back the chocolate.

'Ah, yes.' He wrapped the foil back around the remaining squares and put them in his pocket.

Quite. Exactly. Well, I'm sure you think there can't have been much in it. After all, as you say, he'd only just met her. But these were strange times. That war, it did strange things to all of us. Take me for example. Never had much of a taste for chocolate before. Wasn't much around, of course, but then in the war, with rationing, it became like gold. It wasn't just scarce, it was rare; it was being kept from us. So when you *did* get to have some, well, the taste of it was enriched a thousand times with all those days and months of *not* having it. I've been addicted ever since.

It was like this for Matthew, I think, when he saw Branwen. There'd been a girl in Ireland but that had ended when he'd left to come here and volunteer. In fact, her letter got here before he did. It was waiting for him when he arrived at the hostel address he'd given her. Since then there'd been nobody really. The odd roll in the hay with a certain Sicilian farm girl, but nothing else.

That piece of shrapnel damaged more than just Matthew's leg you see, and it took away more than just a lump of flesh and the cleanness of his stride. It tore out a chunk of his confidence too; that part of a young man's mind that blankets his fears and makes him bold in the face of the enemy, or of a beautiful woman. So yes, Matthew had been lonely in London, very lonely. And he'd seen so much death. In the last four years he'd been surrounded by so much death. In Africa, in Sicily, in Italy, in the hospital in Kent and even here in London once those V1s and V2s started raining down. That changes a man too, you know. Gives him a different outlook on life. For Matthew, it mostly made him assume it wouldn't be going on much longer; that he simply might not be here next week, next month, next year. Quite a thing for a young man to feel, that, especially in his twenties when he should be feeling invincible, as if mortality is a disease to which everyone else is susceptible but to which he and he alone carries a secret immunity.

Now this is where Branwen changed things for Matthew. Her face, her casual, confident manner, her voice, the way she moved, the way she poured that tea, the way her eyes shone under her withheld tears; all of it made him think of death again, but in a different way. She made him want to cheat it for as long as possible, to grab every second of life that was available to him, to take every experience, every change in light on a hillside, every precious breath he breathed in and she breathed out, and hoard and treasure all of it, every day, against that inevitable darkness waiting for them both, just over the horizon.

So, you're right, yes it was quick. And perhaps it was just a young man's lust for a beautiful girl after all. But under the conditions of that war I don't think it would have mattered even if it was. Whatever lit the spark for Matthew isn't important, it was what he wanted to do with that flame, that heat, that's what mattered, and that's where you should judge him. And as for Branwen, well it was quick for her too you know. For all her sassiness, for all her briskness with Matthew that morning, for all her mocking eyebrows and mouth, it hit her just as fast as it hit him. When she left the farmhouse to walk up the hill that morning, her heart was palpitating against her ribs too. Beating and fluttering in there like a panicked bird in a cage; that's how she described it to Matthew, just three days later.

They were watching a magpie at the time, caught in Ben's trap. The birds had been getting at his hens' eggs, and at the eyes of the weaker lambs too, so Ben had set up a trap. First he caught a female as she was feeding on some seed he'd thrown down. Then he put her in one side of a crude wire cage. The other side of this cage was entered through a funnel constructed as to allow a bird in, but not out. Male birds, attracted by the female, would trap themselves inside the second half of the cage, where they'd remain until Ben came to break their necks with one practised twist, like he was unscrewing two halves of a pipe, or wringing out a dishcloth.

For the last three days Matthew had seen hardly anything of Ben. He'd heard his heavy footsteps in the corridor in the morning, heard him leave the house and then seen him at lunch and supper but never in between. Although he always claimed he was working on a fence, or going over to another farm for some piece of equipment, Matthew couldn't help thinking it was more as if he was keeping out of the way on purpose.

Branwen had been right about the two weeks. That was how long Ben wanted to wait before going up to look at the raven nests higher in the mountain. On Matthew's second morning Ben took a letter he'd written to Seybridge explaining the delay into town and posted it back to London. Suddenly, for the first time since his hospitalisation Matthew had nothing to do. His days, expanded with the free, unfilled minutes, stretched out luxuriously before him. He slept late, listened to the radio broadcasts and read a novel he'd brought with him. Mostly, though, he walked, as best he could, up into the hills, helped Branwen with her daily chores or simply waited in some suntrap around the farm for when he could be with her again. On his third day, after he'd helped her usher the two dairy cows back out from the milking shed, he'd suggested they take a walk together instead.

'Where to?' she said.

'Nowhere.'

'Nowhere? Oh, and how exactly do we get there then?'

'Alright, not nowhere,' Matthew had admitted, his palms held up in surrender. 'But just somewhere.'

'Somewhere?' She cocked her head on one side, mock suspicious.

'Actually no,' he corrected himself. 'Not somewhere. Let's just walk.' He dropped his voice in a tone of exaggerated self-pity. 'There was a time,' he said, lowering his head too and putting his hand over the scar on his hip. 'When I thought I never would.'

'A cheap trick, Mr O'Connell,' Branwen said as she strode away from him. 'A dirty, cheap trick.'

'But effective,' Matthew said to himself as he followed her. 'Very effective.'

It was on the way back from that walk they'd come across the trapped magpie, squawking and flapping inside the cage.

'Poor thing,' Branwen had said, keeping her distance.

The bird seemed to hear a hint of hope in her empathy, and with a two-legged hop it tried to fly out of the cage, beating its wings against the wire.

Which was when she told him.

'Tha's how my heart was,' she said quietly, not taking her eyes off the trapped bird. 'That mornin', when I left you. Like it was a bird in there. All the way up the hill, an' for a good hour after too.'

She turned to face him then and saw he'd understood. They hadn't said anything to each other for the past three days, not because they didn't want to, or because they'd been too shy, but simply because they hadn't needed to. They'd both known. She always, from the very first moment he'd stepped down those stairs, and he for certain when, later, they'd said goodnight and her eye had held his for what felt like a delicious eternity.

'That song,' Matthew said now, laying his hands gently on her shoulders and looking down at her. 'The one you were singing before I came in. What's it called?'

'*Ar Lan Y Môr*,' she said. 'Down by the Sea.' Then she shook her head and laughed, just as she had during their first conversation. 'Silly really. Never even seen the sea.'

'It's a beautiful song,' Matthew said, giving her shoulders a squeeze. 'And you sing it beautifully.'

'Thank you Mr O'Connell,' she said, trying to joke her way past the sensations rising in her.

'And if you'll let me,' he continued. 'I'll show you the sea. The Irish Sea. I'll show it to you and then I'll take you over it, to Ireland.' He paused, breathing out a deep breath. 'If you'll let me?'

She looked away at the magpie in the cage, caught within its wires. 'Yes,' she said eventually. 'I'd like that. *Ar Lan Y Môr gyda ti*. Down by the sea,' she continued, looking back at him with the sky's light in her eyes. 'With you.'

That night was the first night Matthew and Branwen spent together, Branwen tiptoeing down the corridor to Matthew's room at the other end of the farm. In the morning, before dawn, she crept back and slept for an hour more, missing the warmth of his body already, then rose to set about making breakfast as usual.

She needn't have bothered with the creeping around. Ben had lived all his life in that farm and, with the weight of him, he'd come to know its every creak and groan, the timbre and pitch of every shifting sigh. He'd lain in his bed that night and, through his ears, had seen clearly the image of his sister's small, bare feet padding down the narrow corridor. In the hour before dawn he'd heard them pad back. The sound of them made him roll lazily onto his front, his own big feet hanging off the end of the bed and an equally large grin buried in his pillow.

Ben still managed, somehow, to appear surprised when Branwen and Matthew sat him down at the kitchen table a week later and told him they were in love. Ben had mentioned over lunch that he thought he'd go and have a look at the raven nests the next day; that he thought it might be time. Once he'd gone off on his afternoon's work, patching a piece of hedge in the paddock, Branwen and Matthew fell immediately into an urgent discussion. The way Matthew saw it, they had no choice. It was now or never. Once Ben had the birds he'd have to return to London. The country was at war, anything could happen. Matthew didn't want to leave without her and she didn't want to see him go. So they decided to tell Ben their plans that night and ask him, as her older brother, for his blessing. Which, after his strained mock surprise, is exactly what Ben gave them, drawing them to him and wrapping them in his huge arms, repeating again and again, 'Wonderful news, wonderful news. *Diolch i Dduw, diolch i Dduw,*' the words reverberating through his massive ribcage into their cheeks, pressed against his chest.

Holding Branwen's hand, openly now, above the table, Matthew earnestly explained his intentions to Ben. He would never, he said, trying to appear more mature than he felt, dream of taking his sister away from him, away from her home without giving both of them his deepest commitment.

'Before we leave,' Matthew said, looking towards Branwen for courage, 'we would like to marry.' He looked into Ben's broad, weather-beaten face. 'I'd like to ask your permission Ben, if I may, to make your sister my wife.'

At first Ben said nothing. He just sat there, nodding his head slowly, as he did when impressed by a particularly fine ram at the local show. Then he smiled, a huge smile that took over his face. 'Of course,' he said. 'Of course. I'll speak to Davies the chapel tomorrow.' Then he looked towards his uncharacteristically silent sister. 'Bran?'

Their eyes met, and as they did Branwen gave a tight, almost imperceptible nod, as if any greater movement would spill something inside her.

'Well,' Ben said through a sigh. 'There it is then. I'll see if we can't have it done the day after tomorrow, Friday.' He stood up, straightening himself to his full height so his hair brushed against the lower beams of the ceiling, and extended his hand towards Matthew. 'Congratulations Mr O'Connell,' he said. 'You're engaged to the most beautiful woman in Wales. I might be biased, of course,' he continued with a wink as Matthew shook his hand, 'but there you go.'

'Thank you,' Matthew said. 'Thank you Ben.' And never before had he meant those words more.

The next day, as Ben rode over to see Davies the minister, Branwen spent hours fretting over leaving her brother to fend for himself. She made out lists of what he should buy, where, from whom and for how much. She wrote out what she did around the house for whoever Ben found to come and help him run the place. Matthew, meanwhile, did what he could to reassure her, while also gently advising her on what to pack for their journey which would take her not just to London, but Ireland too. He'd already decided he would resign from the PWE and take her home. London was no place for her, not with the war, and no place to bring a love as new as theirs either. The prospect of Ireland, meanwhile, had gained a sudden allure for Matthew. He had a strong desire for Branwen to know where he was from, in every way. With her at his side he would no longer be just the returning wounded soldier, the disgraced son. He would be a young husband bringing home his new wife. And Ireland would be his gift to Branwen too. The Irish hills, the smell and salt air of the sea, these were what he would give her. A new country yet familiar in its rhythms and colour to her own.

For Branwen, the idea of Ireland at once excited and scared her. Here she was, twenty-one and never left Wales, about to see London and then leave the whole island of Britain altogether, to travel over a sea she'd never seen to a country she only knew through the accent and stories of her fiancé.

When Ben came back later that afternoon he told them Davies would be expecting them at the old mountain chapel the next morning. They spent the rest of the day unpacking and airing Branwen's mother's wedding dress which had been folded away when she herself was just twenty-one for exactly this day, when her daughter would lift it out and hold it to the light once more. At the same time Ben rooted out an old suit of Evan's which fitted Matthew just about well enough for him to wear it for the ceremony the next day.

That night Ben heard no padding of feet. Matthew and Branwen were, he was pleased to hear, sleeping as a young man and woman should on the eve of their wedding day. Apart and yet together, connected by threads of anxiety, excitement and absence running between them like fine-spun silver, all the way down the length of that night-filled corridor.

When Matthew arrived downstairs for breakfast the next morning he discovered what looked like a large box in the middle of the kitchen table, a grey woollen blanket draped heavily over its edges. Ben was standing beside the range, his face ruddy with early morning air, drinking a mug of tea.

'There you go,' he said with a nod towards the table. 'Six raven chicks, as ordered. Strong little buggers too.'

He took a sip of his tea and Matthew saw his knuckles and the backs of his hands were marked with fresh scratches and cuts. Taking the chicks obviously hadn't been the easiest of tasks.

'Can I take a look?' Matthew asked, approaching the table.

'Just a peek,' Ben said. 'They've only jus' settled. Don't want to get 'em all worked up again.'

Matthew lifted one corner of the blanket and

peered into the wire cage underneath. He could just make out the six chicks inside. Their oversized beaks seemed too heavy for their small heads as they huddled together on a bed of straw, their new feathers, although deeply black, somehow managing to shine with faint purples and blues too. The light from the lifted corner caused them to shuffle and shift, as if a breeze had blown across them, ruffling their feathers.

Matthew lowered the blanket again; silently thanking these birds for their sacrifice which had led him to his love. 'Do you get white ones?' he asked Ben. 'Like in Branwen's name?'

Ben raised his eyebrows in reply. 'Oh yes,' he said. 'They do turn up, sometimes. Only ever seen a couple myself mind, an' only one of 'em was alive.' He looked out of the kitchen window at the brightening spring day outside. 'Beautiful to look at,' he continued. 'Beautiful birds. Completely white they were, pale beaks an' legs even. Bright blue eyes, like opals. Beautiful.'

'They sound it,' Matthew said.

'Too beautiful,' Ben continued, looking back at him. 'Never survive see?'

'Why not?'

'Well, their parents don't feed them do they? Chick like that suddenly thrown up in the nest, lookin' so different. Scares 'em I reckon. They kick 'em out, an' then they starve soon enough.' He took a sip from his tea. 'Ravens jus' meant to be black I suppose, an' tha's how it is. Shame though, 'cause like I say, they're beautiful birds to see.'

'Yes,' Matthew said. 'I imagine they are. I'd like to see one myself one day.'

'Well, no need for that is there?' Ben said, suddenly smiling and pushing himself off the range. 'You're marrying your own aren't you? Talkin' of which, I'd better get that horse of yours ready. If I know Davies 'e'll have been waitin' at the chapel since dawn.' And with that Ben left the house, calling over his shoulder as he went, 'Tell that bride of yours there's a fresh pot on the range an' some bacon on the shelf an' this is the last time her brother'll ever be makin' her breakfast!'

Just a few hours later Matthew and Branwen were riding Mullie back to the farm as newly married man and wife. Ben rode beside them on his own horse, a sturdy Welsh mountain that he rode bareback, his long legs dangling down so far the toecaps of his boots were darkened damp from the mountain's spring grasses. He'd decorated Mullie for the occasion, weaving early honeysuckle and late blossom through his bridle and mane, and sprigs of young hazel through his tail. Branwen rode sitting sideways before Matthew, an arm around his waist. Her mother's wedding dress, which she'd pinned at the back to make it fit perfectly at the front, fell in layers of white silk over Mullie's shoulder as far as his knee. Both man and wife still carried a deep ache within their chests, a hollowing resonance of the emotions stirred up by the ceremony that had joined their lives forever.

Davies had indeed been waiting at the chapel, a small, whitewashed building with one narrow, high-arched, unstained window. Though the chapel itself was simple, its setting gave it the grandeur of a cathedral, perched as it was beneath another sweep of mountain cutting a swathe of green through the high blue sky. A single yew tree spread its shade over a little graveyard of keening gravestones, laid irregularly across the sheep-cropped lawn like abandoned chessmen. Inside, the chapel's thick walls held a sacred coolness, its still space ordered by just six lines of dark pews and a wooden, unadorned pulpit. Davies officiated in Welsh but shadowed his sentences with English, while Ben both gave his sister away and performed the role of Matthew's best man, giving him their mother's wedding ring with which to make his sister his wife. The ring hung so loose on Branwen's slim finger she had to hold her hand in a fist all the way home. They sang one hymn together in English, 'Guide me O thou great Jehovah', then Ben and Branwen sang 'Calon Lân' in Welsh, her clear, high voice harmonising over his bass like a single lark over the broad back of the mountain.

When the new couple walked out of the chapel arm in arm, Matthew's wrists showing long from

Evan's too-short suit, Ben showered them with more blossom before lifting his sister up into the arms of her new husband, already mounted on Mullie. The horse gave one of his snorts as she shifted herself into place, hopefully, Matthew thought, in approval rather than protest.

It was Ben who saw the smoke first, thin grey clouds of it blowing away from the farm's chimney. He knew he'd left some coal smouldering in the range, and that the fire on the other side was unmade. There was no way the coal was making that smoke more than three hours later. He said nothing about it, but then Branwen saw it too. They exchanged a quick glance but remained silent, choosing to let Matthew continue with his reminiscence about how Mullie reminded him of a pony he'd had as a boy. As they neared the farm, however, the horses sliding their hooves down the slope at its back, Matthew noticed the smoke too.

'Look,' he said pointing at the grey wisps dragging away on the breeze. 'Someone's made the fire.'

'Well,' Ben said, employing a mock surprise for the

second time in as many days. 'So they have. Who can that be then?'

It was as if Evan had somehow heard his brother's question. At that very moment his gaunt, tanned face appeared in the corner of one of the farm's lower windows. As they rode closer it stayed there, hung within the glass like a slipped portrait.

'Evan!' As soon as she saw him Branwen was slipping off Mullie's back and, gathering her dress in her hands, running towards the farm as fast as she could, crying out her brother's name again and again. 'Evan! Evan! Is that really you? *Ble wyt ti wedi bod?*'

Matthew watched as Evan's face faded from the window then reappeared, attached to a lean body in uniform at the farm's opened back door. Branwen ran straight into her brother's arms and flung her own around his neck, squealing with joy. Evan's stern expression, staring grimly over her shoulder, didn't change. He just continued looking at Matthew, his hard grey eyes locked on this strange man wearing his own suit, bringing his sister home in their mother's wedding dress.

'*'Pwy yw'r dyn hwn?*' Evan asked Ben over his sister's shoulder.

'*Siarada Saesneg nawr Evan,*' Ben said, dismounting from his horse.

'*Pam?*' Evan replied aggressively.

'Because English is the language of your sister's new husband,' Ben replied in an overly cheerful manner.

Slipping her arms from his neck Branwen leant back to look at her younger brother, a hopeful, worried smile straining her delicate features.

Evan returned her look for a moment before deliberately placing his hands on her shoulders to push her, painfully slowly, away. 'This how you welcome your brother home is it?' he said in English. 'By marrying a stranger without my knowin'?'

Ben went to hand Matthew the reins of his horse but Matthew, as Branwen's new husband, wanted to be the one to heal this sudden wound. Passing Mullie's reins to Ben he stepped forward and, slipping one hand around Branwen's waist, extended his other towards her brother.

'Let me introduce myself,' he said. 'This must be quite a surprise for you. I'm Matthew, Matthew O'Connell. It's an honour to meet you.'

Evan didn't take Matthew's offered hand but just looked him hard in the face, the muscles around his jaw and eye sockets twitching like the flank of a pony under the touch of summer flies. Then his eyes dropped to Matthew's other hand, resting on his sister's hip, before coming back to meet his face again.

'A neutral bloody Irishman too.' The way he screwed that second word through his lips, as if it was painful to speak, made the word anything but neutral. Shaking his head he turned away to walk into the darkness of the house.

'I'll speak with him,' Ben said, appearing at Matthew's shoulder and giving him the reins of both horses. 'Don't worry *bach*,' he said to Branwen, giving her arm a squeeze. 'He'll come round now, you'll see.'

While Ben went inside to talk with his younger brother, Matthew and Branwen untacked the horses and put them out into the paddock to graze. As they did Matthew tried his best to reassure his young wife she shouldn't worry too much about Evan's reaction. They'd no idea he was coming home. If they had, they'd have waited of course. And, he told her, she shouldn't take anything he says now, when he's only just returned, with too much weight. 'God knows,' he said softly, holding her to him. 'We all leave too much of ourselves behind in this war, and bring back more of it than we should too. He'll have seen some things out there,' he continued, stroking her hair (and done some things too no doubt, he'd thought to himself) 'which can change a man for a while. But not for ever Bran, you'll see now, not for ever. I promise.'

A couple of hours later the four of them were sitting in the sparsely furnished living room next to the kitchen. Ben had lit the fire, more to add a feeling of warmth to the rarely used room than to heat it against the mild spring evening. He'd opened a bottle of his best cider too, to celebrate. From the strain across his broad brow Matthew thought perhaps it might have been wiser to have stayed in the kitchen where they'd eaten supper, rather than invest the evening with even more of a sense of occasion. Not that the meal had passed any more easily. In the face of Evan's sullen disapproval their wedding clothes felt more provocative than celebratory. Ben had done his best to pilot the talk into calmer waters, but to no avail. Every subject seemed mined with explosive potential. They all knew better than to ask Evan about his tour of duty while Matthew's own military experience also seemed like dangerous ground. Matthew had, at least, been able to make it clear that unlike his country he'd also fought in the war. But Evan remained suspicious. 'Wound in the leg was it?' he'd asked pointedly. Matthew knew what he was implying. A leg wound was the most common self-injury to get you out of the war. 'Yes,' he'd replied, allowing more edge to his voice than he'd intended. 'Shrapnel from a '75.'

Now, as they all sat in the living room, Matthew watched Evan as Ben and Branwen did their best to talk the night through to some kind of peace. He sat between them, so much smaller than Ben, coiled and tense, his face still fluttering with that wing of tension beneath his skin. His manner was that of an irritable child who might, at any moment, tip the whole room into sudden awkwardness with a barbed comment or a show of irascible disdain. Matthew recognised all of it; he'd seen it many times before in other men returned from the frontline. Suddenly back in the trappings of their past lives they found the people they'd thought they'd loved, the memories of whom had fortified them through the most terrible and terrifying of times, now turned into hateful monsters of ignorance and normality, apparently uncaring and unaware of what had happened to the world and to the human race we'd once called man.

This was why Matthew only felt angry at Evan for Branwen's sake. For himself he felt nothing but pity for this broken man sitting in the armchair opposite him, still wearing his uniform. Just like that uniform, Matthew knew Evan would also still be wearing the ragged remains of the terrible contradiction in which his country had asked him to cloak himself. The idea that for the last two years the best way he could protect the life he knew was to kill other men. And that now, just a ship's sail later, those same actions would, in the eyes of that same life and his loved ones within it, be the very worst thing he could do as a human being.

Despite this knowledge of what Evan had undergone it was still hard for Matthew to witness the distress her brother's words could inflict upon Branwen. 'Well,' Evan had said to Matthew at one point, when Ben left the room to open another bottle of cider. 'Regular knight in shinin' armour aren't yew? Even got yer own bloody white charger.' He'd flicked his chin towards the window and the paddock beyond, where Mullie was still grazing contentedly.

'Evan!' Branwen admonished him through tensed teeth, her eyes pricking with tears as they had done several times already that evening. 'Please!' Her imploring of him was so desperate, so shot through with genuine pain that it made Matthew's heart bleed to see Evan turn from his sister in response, a sneer disfiguring his lips. So he'd been hugely grateful when Ben, after one more glass of cider, had slapped his thighs and announced, 'Well, time for bed I'd say. Time for bed,' and all of them, except Evan, had stood to say their stilted, disjointed goodnights.

As the newly married couple prepared for bed in Branwen's bedroom, Evan having been given his own room back, the raised voices of her brothers arguing below reached them, muffled and dull, rising from the kitchen beneath. They were arguing in Welsh but Matthew didn't ask Branwen to translate. He just held her in bed instead, her head on his chest as she silently wept, one of his hands over her outward ear and the other stroking her hair as he whispered to her gently, 'shhh now, shhh Bran. It'll be fine, you'll see. I promise it will. I promise.'

It was the screams that woke them. After they'd heard the front door slam shut, bringing an end to the voices rising from below, Matthew and Branwen had lain very still, listening to the silence of the night. Eventually, as this silence eased them back to themselves, they'd begun to make love, quietly and gently, as if the distress of the evening could all too easily be woken again. Afterwards, still lying in each other's arms, they'd fallen into a deep, exhausted sleep. So they hadn't heard Evan return from his long night's walk across the mountain to a front room in the village which served as the nearest pub. And they hadn't heard him emerge from his room a few minutes later either, or the sound of his drunken stumbling as he weaved his way down the corridor, his service bayonet clenched in his hand, to arrive outside their bedroom door, sweating and breathing heavily as he stood there swaying in the dark, bat-tling with the conflicting voices in his head. It was only when he finally, slowly, turned from their door and made his way down the spiral staircase, through the kitchen and out into the paddock, that the sleeping couple were eventually woken.

Mullie's screams were inhuman and yet all too human; high, piercing whinnies of pain, fear and confusion. At first, when Matthew started awake at the sound of them, bolting upright in the bed, he thought he was back on the landing beaches of

Sicily. Branwen was quicker to understand what was happening. Grabbing her husband's arm, she woke with her brother's name already on her lips, 'Evan!'

Fumbling in the darkness, Matthew pulled on his trousers and searched for matches to light an oil lamp. 'Leave it!' Branwen cried at him urgently as another of Mullie's screams tore through the night, echoing against the high rocks of the mountains.

A full moon was shining brightly in a cloudless sky so when Matthew burst from the farm's front door he discovered, as much as he wished he hadn't, that he could see all too clearly what Evan was doing. Ben was already there, standing dumbstruck in his nightshirt, his hair wild with fitful sleep, unable to believe the sight before them in the paddock.

Mullie had fallen to his knees but was still struggling to rise, one foreleg pawing the ground as he tried to lift himself from under the relentless slashes and stabs of Evan's bayonet. Evan had already sliced away the horse's lips, eyelids and ears. He'd also hacked at the base of his tail. Still woven with hazel, it hung from his rump by a few shreds of flesh and hide. His flanks, shoulder and stomach were slashed with deep cuts, gulping with blood, dark in the moonlight.

Matthew only got a few steps beyond the porch before he was stopped dead by the scene. The next thing he knew he was dropping to the floor himself, bent double as he retched on the bile suddenly choking his throat. Matthew's reaction galvanised Ben out of his stunned astonishment. Taking a deep intake of breath to fuel a cry as sudden and terrifying as thunder, he bellowed his brother's name into the night, 'Evan!' before sprinting through the paddock's open gate and into the field to knock Evan flying with one sweep of his massive arm. Looking up, Matthew thought Ben had killed him. Evan lay sprawled in the grass, one of his legs folded awkwardly underneath his hip. But far from killing him, the blow seemed to wake Evan. Lifting himself on one elbow he looked towards his older brother, who was now crouching beside Mullie, cradling the horse's mutilated head in his lap. Matthew was too far away to see Evan's face, previously set in a rigor mortis of violence, fall and collapse, as if the bones inside were melting. He only heard his strangled scream as, like a leaf in a fire, he curled up into himself, crying out the same words again and again through a storm of wracking sobs. They were Welsh words, and it was only several days later that Branwen could bring herself to translate for Matthew what Evan been saying. 'I could smell him!' Evan shouted into the night. 'I could smell him! On the bed! The sheets! I could smell him!'

The sound of Branwen coming through the porch forced Matthew to his feet just in time to catch her at the door and violently push her back into the house. 'Don't!' he found himself shouting at her. 'Don't look! Don't Bran, don't!' But she didn't have to. She already knew what Evan had done and the confirmation she heard in her husband's panicked voice sent her crumpling to her knees in defeat. The next sound the two of them heard, crouched together on the flagstones of the kitchen floor, was the single crack of Ben's rifle as he stood over Mullie to put the horse out of his misery. If only, Matthew would find himself thinking many months later, our own miseries could be dispatched so easily. But they can't. This is what Matthew would learn from that awful night onwards, this was the lesson of which he would be a student for the rest of his life. They can't.

The first light of the following morning seemed to have knowledge of what had happened in its absence. Clouds had filled the sky and the sun shone through them, weak and pale across the mountains, to fall over the same woollen blanket that had covered the ravens, now draped over the disfigured head, neck and shoulders of Mullie's corpse in the paddock. At supper the day before Matthew had thought that maybe they should postpone their journey to London by another day until Evan was more settled with the idea of their marriage. But now, after what he'd witnessed last night, he was resolved. All forgiveness or understanding for Evan had bled from him as quickly as the blood had gulped from those slashes along Mullie's flanks. He and Branwen would leave as soon as they could. They would ride Ben's cart into town and take the ravens back to London where, having completed his task, Matthew would resign from the PWE and take Branwen back to his home in Ireland.

Branwen, still in a state of shock, listened dumbly to her husband as he firmly laid down what they should do, nodding weakly at his most definite intentions. She didn't care anymore; she just wanted someone else to guide her, to tell her where to go, so shattered was her sense of herself, her family and her world.

Ben was harnessing his horse to the cart when Matthew emerged from the farmhouse carrying his own leather case and Branwen's larger trunk of belongings. Evan was still asleep. Matthew wanted to leave before he woke as he didn't know what he might do should he see him again.

Ben had already apologised a hundred times for Evan. This really, he'd urged Matthew to understand, was not his brother. The man who'd done that to the horse, this was someone else, a stranger the war had regurgitated back to them. Someone who wore the face and body of Evan, but no more. Beyond these apologies there'd been little else to say so the two men stuck to the details of the travel arrangements, Ben's decision to stay and bury Mullie and look after Evan, and his advice to Matthew about where to leave the cart so he might pick it up later from town. Now though, as Matthew turned back towards the house, having left their luggage beside the cart, Ben did have something else to say to him.

'Matthew,' he said, stopping him with a hand on his shoulder. 'It's not much of a dowry I know, but I want you to have this.'

Matthew turned round to see Ben holding out a pocket watch in his other hand. The silver casement dangled from a fine link chain wrapped round the big man's fingers.

'It was our grandfather's,' Ben continued as he lowered the watch into Matthew's palm, letting the chain coil down beside it. Matthew looked down at the watch and, pressing the tiny latch, opened the casement to reveal a gold and ivory face inside. It was beautifully made. He could feel the steady tick of its mechanism, faint but certain against his hand, like the heart of a caught songbird. There was something engraved in italics on the inside of the casement lid. *Y Crochan*.

'The moniker of the watchmaker,' Ben said, following Matthew's eyes. '*The Cauldron*. Only put his mark on his very best pieces, an' not many of 'em left now.'

'Thank you,' Matthew said gravely, closing the casement and slipping the watch into his pocket.

'Well,' Ben sighed, looking over to where Mullie lay in the paddock. 'Nothin' in the face of it really. But I wanted to give you somethin' at least.'

Matthew felt a welling of love for this giant of a man he'd only known for three weeks. 'You've given me your sister Ben,' he said laying a hand on his arm. 'She'll always be enough.'

Ben turned back to look at Matthew again. 'I hope so,' he said. 'I hope so. But Matthew?' he continued. 'Do one thing for me will you? That book I gave you. Take it, an' read it too. It was written a long time ago now, I know, but underneath, well, the stories are the same.' He took a step closer to his new brother-in-law. 'We keep telling them, like, in different ways, but they're still the same. An' I reckon they'll go on being so 'til we learn from 'em.'

Matthew nodded and patted Ben's arm, thinking that when Evan cut up the horse he must have sliced his older brother to the bone too. What Ben had seen last night had obviously unsettled him greatly, and left him grasping for old stories as some kind of anchor. 'We'd best be going,' Matthew said turning back for the house. 'I'll get the birds, and tell Bran.'

Ben watched Matthew walk away before returning to buckle the straps of the harness, hoping he'd both said enough, and yet not too much.

Although visions of what Evan had done haunted Branwen nightly, within a few days of leaving the farm the cascade of new experiences began to dull the terrible vividness of the events of her wedding night. First there had been the train through the flat English plains to London, packed with American GIs. Then the capital itself, in all its ravaged beauty;

St Paul's, the Houses of Parliament and of course the Tower itself where she and Matthew saw their raven chicks safely deposited with the Ravenmaster. There were glimpses of her new husband's past life too; the smoky pub where he'd drunk on the way back from work, his landlady, insisting on seeing her wedding ring before allowing her entry to the dingy lodgings. But then, before she knew it, she was heading west again, as far as her first sighting of the sea. As they'd waited for their ferry Matthew had laughed at her, unable as she was to tear her eyes away from the waves belly-flopping to the shore, the spumes of white water and the gulls peeling away from the cliffs above the beaches. And then, on the other side of that great sullen, swaying body of water, there was another country altogether, another train journey and at its end, another farm with Matthew's family, telegraphed in advance, waiting nervously to meet them.

Those first days in Ireland were confusing for Branwen. All at once she was seeing and learning more about her husband's past, but also new facets of his present character too. Matthew had been as nervous as she about his long-postponed return, and over those early days he'd seemed to swing wildly between a great pride in his new wife and an exaggerated, irritable concern over her well-being. She soon realised that she was, in some part, a kind of a peace offering between Matthew and his family. In the face of this beautiful young bride his father had made grudging concessions of appeasement towards his son who had, at least, returned from Britain with something of use. These appeasing gestures were helped along further when, less than a month after their arrival, the D-Day invasions happened. The stories that began filtering out of Europe in their wake couldn't help but cast Matthew's impetuous actions four years earlier in a more understanding light. But all wasn't healed between Matthew and his family. The simple fact that he'd left at all could still pull the air taut between them, while his wounded leg remained the physical reminder Matthew feared it would. Every time he rose to limp awkwardly across the room or down the lane towards the fields, he had to suffer either his father's scowl or, worse, his mother's pitiful tears for her maimed son. Both branded him inside with a scalding burn of suppressed anger and regret.

Despite these residual tensions, Matthew's father tried his best to focus on his son's present return rather than his past departure. It was agreed that Matthew and Branwen should take over a small cottage on the edge of the family farm. The cottage had lain empty for several years now, but Matthew's father had already begun repairing the roof and cutting back the overgrown garden. He gave them the surrounding few acres too and, if Matthew managed these well, then they'd talk further about him taking on more of the land in the future. His father was getting older now and his sisters were already married off so, provided he put his shoulder to the wheel, his father told him, as if he hadn't done a day's work for the last four years, then nothing stood in his way of inheriting the whole farm one day.

To begin with it looked hopeful. Branwen threw herself into making the cottage a home, while Matthew used his army pension to buy new equipment and tools. Both of them relished finally being alone in their own house and there were some weeks, when the sun shone and Matthew's father left them to their own devices, that they were truly happy. Their days took on a shared rhythm and each became the other's anchor, the gravitational body around which their hours orbited. At these times Matthew wanted to be nowhere else other than coming home from the fields, aching with a day's good work, to his beautiful wife singing softly to welcome him home at the gate of their autumnal cottage. For Branwen's part, although she missed Ben and the farm in the hills, she was invigorated by this challenge of a new country, family and home. She wrote to Ben, and to Evan too who, under his brother's careful eye, seemed to be beginning to find the parts of himself he'd lost overseas. From day to day, though, Branwen tried not to think of Wales too much, determined as she was to focus her love upon Matthew and the distress that return to his own home was clearly causing him.

Within a few months that distress had grown into more persistent problems. The cottage was isolated but Matthew and Branwen could only live there through interaction with the village where they bought and sold produce and where they got their only news and entertainment. Branwen's beauty, which had seemed such a prize on their arrival, soon became a thorn in the sides of many of the local women. They eyed her delicate features, her poise, her dark hair, with suspicion, as if anyone this beautiful on the outside had to be hiding an ugliness within. That, at least, is what they said to each other. In private they knew it was the eyes of their own husbands that fed their distrust, the way they lingered a second too long over Branwen when she came in to market. Or, even worse, how they looked at them, their wives, afterwards.

To compound this growing suspicion of his wife Matthew had, while drinking in the village pub one evening, told another farmer what happened on their wedding night. A sober man during the war, Matthew had, since his return, increasingly been finding refuge from his family tensions in drink. On this occasion another argument with his father had sent him to the pub where a quick succession of whiskies loosened his tongue and seduced him into an indulgence of storytelling. Through the lens of those shot glasses he even found a morbid delight in vividly evoking the scene for his enraptured listener; painting for him in gory detail Mullie's earless, lidless, lipless head, the great gashes torn along his sides and the flash of Evan's bayonet in the moonlight.

It didn't take long for the story to spread, or for Branwen to hear it, stage-whispered in the bakery a week later. In the eyes of the village, as Evan's sister the shadow of his crime fell over Branwen too. Those women who'd first suspected her beauty felt themselves, in the wake of this story, somehow justified and said as much, nodding their heads with the weight of their wisdom.

When Branwen returned home that day she was furious. It was the first time Matthew had seen her anger, the first time he'd seen those mountains, rocks and tearing winds of her home come alive in her accusing eyes, in her shrill, shouted voice of betrayal. In the face of her fury he'd accepted her blame and he'd felt his wrongdoing painfully for weeks afterwards. For a time the transgression looked as if it had been just that; no more than a temporary diversion from their true journey together. But then Matthew's attention was taken by another story being whispered through the village; a story not about his wife, but him.

Matthew had returned to Ireland as a spy for the British. That was how the rumour ran. That the war in Europe was as good as done and now the British would be turning their gaze back west, towards Ireland. Matthew, so the story went, was one of many Irish men who'd fought for the British and now been recruited to their cause.

It was preposterous and at first, when his father took him aside to tell him, Matthew had done no more than laugh in disbelief. But as the story passed from ear to ear, so it strengthened, until he began to feel the force of its influence every day. Nothing he said made any difference, no defence he offered seemed capable of damming the story's flow and as the months cooled towards winter Matthew realised, with horror, that the very gossip that had been his trade at the Rumour Mill could all too easily become his undoing.

The village, already suspicious of the rare beauty he'd brought back from Britain, began to turn openly against them. Branwen found herself shouldered out of conversations in the market, while Matthew increasingly found himself sitting alone on his nights in the pub. His own parents, fearing the community more than the abandonment of their son, became distant and although only half a mile up the lane may as well have been living in Dublin for all they saw of them.

As the year turned, as the nights drew in, and the coastal salt winds harried the land, so a turning began in Matthew too. The new confidence he'd found in marrying Branwen was gradually unpicked and unravelled by both his drinking and the village's endless gossip. The combined pressure of these, the fog and depression of the drink, the cruel claustrophobia of the gossip, pressed in with ever greater force upon Matthew's already fragile mind. Within just a few months of first hearing that rumour about him being a spy, Matthew, in desperation and without knowing it, began to side with the village against his wife.

At first it was in such a way as neither of them noticed. But side with them he did, subtly, within himself, to save himself. Through a confused haze of fear, drink and insecurity, Matthew began to blame Branwen, the victim of the villagers' scorn, for their situation, rather than the perpetrators themselves.

As Matthew had said that day they'd ridden back from the chapel to find Evan so twisted up with anger, most men returning from the war brought back more of it than they should. But not all showed the change as immediately as Evan had that night. For Matthew, it seems, the years of war, the ravaging of his leg, the months in that dark basement in blitz-broken London, all of it finally began to surface through him now, over that long cold winter in Ireland. A slow seepage of regret and hate that spread through his body to gradually infect every part of him. It was his hate for the gossiping, ignorant villagers, for his father, blinded by prejudice, for Evan's sneering disdain and even for the wider world which had allowed all this to happen. All of this found an outlet in his turning against Branwen. For what? He couldn't say. For being the innocent cause of their pain? For making him fall in love with her in the first place? He had no answer, and often he felt as if he were watching another man treat her the way he did; sullenly refusing to speak with her, leaving a room when she entered, retreating more and more to the company of a bottle when he knew she ached for his touch and loving word. It wasn't that he no longer found her attractive, he did. Or that he no longer loved her. Again, he thought that he did. It was, if anything, as much a turning from himself as from her. A spiteful refusal to reach for the one true note in his out-of-tune life; a refusal tragically strengthened, rather than weakened, when Branwen gave birth to their son.

Branwen already knew she was pregnant when

she'd arrived in Ireland, although she'd waited another month before she told Matthew. She'd hoped the birth of their son would be a salve to their growing troubles, but it wasn't. On the contrary, Matthew seemed to resent the love and attention his wife lavished on the baby, while his son's open, untouched innocence only made him feel even more damaged by the world. Branwen, lost in the face of her husband's cruelty, moored herself tighter and tighter to her child. It was as if, she thought, she'd been cursed by her own name, and like those white ravens, too different, too beautiful for the nest of their parents, she was being abandoned to suffer and starve on the cold rocks of Matthew's indifference.

Branwen endured a year and a half of this life before she began to consider how she might leave it. Now and then she'd thought she'd seen flickering moments of hope on the horizon; the rare hour when Matthew seemed to come back to himself, a blissful two days without seeing anyone else from the village or the area. But these had always been brief and ungrounded on any real change in their situation. Soon, she knew there was no hope and, for the sake of herself and for her young son, she began to look for a way to return to Wales.

They had no telephone in the cottage and any letters she'd ever sent home were posted over the counter at the village post office. Now, with the way things had turned, this was the last thing she wanted to do. Someone there was bound to tell Matthew she'd written home to Wales and, as bitter as he'd become, he'd want to know why she was writing and to whom. No, she had to find another way to let Ben know how lonely and scared she was, how much she wanted to return to the farm and to escape from her husband who, though she still loved him, she no longer recognised.

The thread of an opportunity finally blew her way one morning the next summer. She'd been down at the village's small harbour buying fish from the fresh catch brought in the night before. Having once again suffered the cold shoulders of the other women Branwen was about to begin pushing her son's pram up the winding lane back to their cottage when, suddenly, she heard a scrap of Wales blown her way on the air. She stopped and listened. Yes, there it was again, more clearly this time. It was a song, the same one she'd sung that morning when Matthew had first come down those stairs for breakfast, *Ar Lan Y Môr*. Turning the pram around she followed the voice, a man's smooth baritone, back down to the far end of the harbour where, at the very end of the jetty, she saw the singer. He was a young man working on a small seiner, untangling a heap of nets spread over its cramped deck. The boat's name was painted in red over its green-washed planks, *Y Ddrudwen*. Taking a deep breath for courage, Branwen pushed the pram on, calling out when close enough, '*Mae'n dda i glywed cân o gartref!*'

The young fisherman, Alun, had been all too happy to stop in his work and talk with this pretty young mother, to speak Welsh across the sea from his home. He was, he told Branwen, from Fishguard, but now and then when the tides were in his favour and the weather was good he'd dock along the Irish coast and sell his catch here, before setting out to fish again on his way home to Wales. An hour later Branwen was waving Alun goodbye, promising herself, as she watched his boat pitch and roll on the waves, that from now on she'd always walk this way on fine days, on the chance of meeting him again.

For many weeks Branwen found excuses to make that walk down to the harbour. Despite her searching of the bobbing boats though, she never heard Alun singing, and each time she returned to the cottage with the letter she'd written to Ben still folded in the pocket of her skirt. After two months of repeating this pattern she began to think Alun and his boat had been no more than just another false horizon, another taunting possibility faded out of sight.

But then, one August morning, when the sun was turning the choppy sea to diamonds, Branwen walked to the harbour once more and, this time, heard Alun's voice again, rising and falling over the buckets of fish, the mounds of nets and the boats tugging on their moorings. '*Ar lan y môr mae rhosys cochion.*' The words brought tears to her eyes and, fearful she'd somehow miss him, that he was at that very minute piloting his seiner out of the harbour, Branwen broke into a run, pushing her son's pram before her. To her relief Alun was exactly where she'd found him before, mending his nets on the deck of *Y Ddrudwen*, moored at the end of the jetty. An hour of talking later and Branwen was pushing her son's pram back up the lane towards home, still humming the song's tune, the pocket of her skirt empty.

The first Matthew knew of the letter Branwen had written, and the first Branwen knew that Alun had actually posted it and hadn't, as she'd feared, lost it overboard or among the tangle of nets on his boat, was a single firm knock on the front door of their cottage which, ever since they'd lived there, had never been knocked on before.

Branwen was playing with her son who, having discovered his walking legs several months earlier, was now tottering back and forth between his mother's chair beside the fire and the edge of the table. Matthew was sitting in an armchair on the other side of the fireplace, reading his paper and listening to a radio news report about the aftermath of Japan's official surrender following that summer's bombing of Hiroshima and Nagasaki. America's use of those terrifying new weapons had, in the weeks since, sent him even deeper into himself, as if the world, once again, had proved it would only ever meet violence with greater violence; that even in the name of good, evil would always be done.

The single knock caught both Matthew and Branwen by surprise. For a moment they just looked at each other as their son continued to shuttle between the chair and the table, giggling to himself at the amazement of this new-found feat. Eventually, folding his paper, Matthew rose from his chair and went to the door. Branwen strained to listen, a sudden cocktail of emotions coursing through her body. From just the depth of that one heavy knock she knew it was Ben at the door. But simultaneous with that knowledge was an instant confusion as to whether she should be dismayed or overjoyed by its sound. She looked around the little room of the cottage which, with the fire roaring, a crisp autumn night at the windows, the folded paper on the arm of the chair, looked, without Matthew's sullen presence, like the picture of domestic fidelity. And even with him there, had it really been so bad this evening? They'd had a better day than usual. Matthew had, as ever, been sombre and while he hadn't exactly been kind to her, he hadn't exactly been unkind either. Then she saw her son, their son, his face already budding with Matthew's features. He was toddling back on another lap to her chair. When he reached her she kept hold of him, telling him gently to 'shhh now *cariad*' as she continued to strain for a sound from the door.

The first voice she heard was her older brother's deep bass, resonant with determination. 'We've come for Branwen, Matthew.'

Then her husband's, slow, steady response, failing, despite his effort, to smooth out the waver of surprise in his reply. 'Ben. Evan. Come in, let's talk.'

Matthew limped back into the room, looking suddenly pale. Throwing Branwen a pleading glance, he made way for her brothers to enter behind him. And then, there they were, Ben's massive frame bowing through the door into the living room and Evan, the tan of Burma shed from his skin, but the nervous tick still flicking there underneath. They'd left the same day they'd received her letter and had been travelling for two whole days. They still wore the farm clothes they'd been wearing when the letter arrived and had brought nothing with them other than a bag of bread and cheese and some water for the journey. At least, this is what Ben thought. Unknown to him Evan had also packed a Nambu Japanese service pistol. He'd taken it off the body of an Imperial Army officer in Burma and had carried it all the way back to Wales. Now, concealed in his jacket pocket, he'd brought it to this cottage in Ireland.

'Won't you sit?' Matthew said, trying to sound as welcoming as possible. 'You must be hungry. Can we get you something to eat?'

'No,' Ben said sternly. 'We won't stay. We'll be leaving now, once Bran has packed her things.'

Turning to his sister, he said in Welsh '*Dyna beth wyt ti eisiau, ynte Bran?*'

'What did you say to her?' Matthew said, suddenly panicked.

'I asked her if that's what she still wanted Matthew.'

'Still? What do you mean still?' Matthew turned to Bran, but she lowered her head to her son instead. Unused to seeing anyone in the cottage other than his parents, and anyone at all the size of Ben, the boy had backed into his mother for refuge, hiding his face in her skirt.

'I gave you your chance Matthew,' Ben said. 'You said my sister would always be enough for you. But she hasn't been has she?'

Ben's great height and size, which Matthew had always thought of as being so benevolent, were now, imbued as they were with his suppressed anger, truly threatening. Sensing her husband's rising panic, and wanting to speak before Evan said anything flamable, Branwen spoke to Matthew, as gently as she could.

'It doesn't have to be forever Matthew. Just a few

months maybe. But I do need... I do have to…'

'Forever?' Matthew snapped back at her. 'Forever? We were meant to be forever, have you forgotten that Bran?'

'Don't speak to her like that!' Evan burst out, stepping towards Matthew.

'Evan, *paid*!' Ben said, blocking his brother with his arm. But it was too late. The raised voices, the edge of anger in the air, it was all too much for the little boy. Realising for the first time in his young life that his new-found legs might be used not just for play, but also to take him away from that which frightened him, he slipped free of his mother's arms and made for the door. Ben tried to bend and catch him but his height made him too slow. Evan was quicker and, making a lunge for the toddler, almost caught him. Another inch closer and he would have grabbed him. That was all it would have taken; an inch, no more, and this story might have ended differently. As it was Evan's hand grasped at thin air before making contact with the boy's running leg, tripping him headlong into the open fire.

With the instincts of a mother Branwen was instantly both screaming and lifting her son from the flames at once. But the boy's jumper was already alight, the wool catching like dried tinder, sending a combustion of flames raging the length of his arm. In the following seconds many things happened at once. Ben dived to help his sister, smothering the flames eating his nephew's arm with his huge hands. Matthew, already outraged at just the sight of him, went for Evan. Evan, with the instincts of Burma still woven into his fabric, drew his pistol.

The shot sent Matthew flying across the room. He landed heavily, thudding onto his back behind the table. Suddenly, in the wake of the gunshot's ear-splitting crack, the only sound was the boy, crying and writhing in pain and fear. The three adults around him were all silent and frozen, Ben and Branwen both staring in shock at the smoking barrel of Evan's pistol and Evan himself also looking down at the gun, as if it were held in another man's hand and not his own. Confusion and alarm ran through his features like a sudden gust through a field of wheat. Lifting his head, the first thing he saw was Matthew's motionless legs protruding from behind the table, then the faces of his brother and sister, transformed in shock and disbelief. He watched, as if through a thick pane of glass, as Branwen turned, painfully slowly, towards the prone body of her husband, and witnessed the terrible transfiguring of grief, her expression contorting into a silent, choking scream of horror.

Something in Evan's own features must have betrayed the wave of thought arriving in him then; the sudden realisation that must have felt, however fleetingly, like the only thing left for him to do. Even before he'd started lifting his arm Ben was already rising from where he'd been crouched beside the boy, shouting his brother's name once more, 'Evan!' as loudly as he had that night he'd run into the paddock and knocked him from his feet with a single blow. But for the second time that evening Ben wasn't quick enough, and there was nothing he could do as Evan slid the barrel of the pistol into his mouth and pulled the trigger.

It was the sound of that second shot that dragged Matthew back to consciousness. The bullet Evan had fired at him had penetrated his waistcoat and hit the casement of the silver pocket watch Ben had given him the morning they'd left the farm. Piercing the casement the bullet had shattered the inner workings but hadn't gone any further, spreading and flattening into a splash of lead instantly welded to the delicate cogs, springs and pins of the watch's mechanism.

The force of the impact had still been considerable, knocking Matthew out, breaking one of his ribs and sending a crushing shockwave through his chest and lungs. The sound of the second shot reached him like a distant echo, a vague hand, shaking him awake. As the light seeped back into his eyes, as he became aware of where he was once more, Matthew tried to speak. When he did, he found he couldn't. Hearing the commotion in the room, but unable to see it; hearing the hysterical cries of his wife and the cries of his son, Matthew tried to bring words to his lips, but none would come. He tried to move, but again found he could not. His eyes were open and despite the sound of the shot still ringing in his ears, he could hear. He could even smell the tang of cordite from the fired pistol, and the charring of his waistcoat where the bullet had entered. But his body and his voice were paralysed, silenced by the bullet cooling in the distorted workings of his watch.

Lying there, on the floor, his vision limited to the ceiling above him, Matthew listened as Ben, speaking urgently in rushed Welsh, hurried Branwen and their son out of the house. He heard him gathering together clothes for them and then the sound of him physically carrying them both from the room and on, out of the front door.

Just as Branwen's voice had been the first thing Matthew had known of his wife, her singing rising through the floorboards beneath his bed, so her voice would be the last he'd know of her too. As his sight began to fade again, Matthew could still make out Branwen's pitiful repeated moan as her brother carried her into the night. 'Matthew, Matthew, Matthew,' was all she said. His name, diminishing into the distance before echoing again in his mind, 'Matthew, Matthew, Matthew,' as his eyes dimmed and the light within them extinguished to darkness.

When it was clear the old man wasn't going to continue, Rhian spoke. 'But,' she said. 'He wasn't dead was he?'

She'd asked a question, but said it as a statement. The old man turned to look at her. Her forehead was. creased in thought, and he saw that she knew. 'No,' he said, 'he didn't die. But then, he's never really been alive since either.'

'How d'yer mean?'

'Well,' the old man said with a sigh. 'Matthew's father heard those shots and arrived at the cottage soon after Ben and Branwen had left. He called the police straight away, of course, finding his son lying there, and Evan too; the back of his head blown away. The police took Matthew to hospital where they fixed up his rib as best they could. An inspector came back the next day to question him. Matthew's voice and some of his movement had come back by then. Propped up in his bed he told the inspector everything, but said he didn't want to press any charges for abduction or for anything else. The only people to have committed any crimes, he told the inspector, had been himself and Evan, he saw that now. He against Branwen's love, Evan against them all. Evan had taken care of his own punishment and so would Matthew. That's what he promised himself as he lay there in that hospital bed. A week later he was discharged, first to his parents' house and then, a week later again, to his own silent cottage where he walked through its front door still carrying a bruise the size of a tennis ball over his heart.

When he opened that door Matthew found a letter waiting for him on the mat. It had arrived that same morning and although he didn't recognise the handwriting he knew exactly who and where it was from. Sitting down beside the fireplace, the ash from that fateful night still piled beneath the grate, he opened the letter and read. It was from Ben. He'd heard about Matthew's survival when he'd read a newspaper article about Evan's suicide. But the paper had run the story too late. Ben had bought the copy when he was in town, having just left the hospital where he'd listened to the coroner read his report in a room off the mortuary where Branwen's body was laid out. The best diagnosis the coroner had been able to give, Ben wrote, was that Branwen had died of a broken heart.

Later that night, after Matthew had cried himself dry, he went to the bookshelf and pulled out the copy of the *Mabinogion* Ben had told him to read. Sitting on the bed he'd shared with his wife, surrounded by her clothes, by what he could still salvage of her scent, Matthew read the Second Branch, the myth of Branwen, Daughter of Llyr. When he'd finished the story he understood. He wrote back to Ben that night, telling him he would follow this letter he was sending to Wales. He wanted to lay flowers on Branwen's grave and to retrieve their son. But when Matthew did journey back to that little town in the hills there was already a reply from Ben waiting for him with the stationmaster. The note told Matthew where to find Branwen's grave within the grounds of the mountain chapel where they'd married. But then it also asked him not to visit the farm, not to come for his son, but to leave them, Ben and his nephew, alone. 'The boy is happy here,' it read. 'Let him be so now.'

Matthew respected Ben's wishes and, against his strongest desires, stayed away from that mountain farmhouse to which he'd brought so much tragedy. He did, though, climb up into the hills to the old chapel where he laid white lilies on Bran's grave, propping them carefully under the inscription on her headstone – '*Llawn yw'r coed o ddail a blode, / Llawn iawn o gariad ydwyf inne.*' 'The woods are full of leaves and flowers / And I am full of love.' Kneeling beside her there, Matthew vowed he would never return home until he'd found a way to make amends to her family, even if that meant never seeing Ireland again.'

This time the old man made it clear he'd come to the end of his story. Sitting back on the bench he sighed, apparently transported by his own words far away from London and the traffic rushing past on the road behind them.

Somehow, the day was already turning. The sun seemed to have quickened through the sky so when Rhian looked at the old man's profile his face was lit in the honeyed light of evening. 'I don't understand,' she said at last. 'How would reading the myth have helped him?'

'Well,' the old man said, leaning forward again and placing his hands on his stick and his chin on his hands. 'Maybe it wouldn't. But those old stories, they're all lessons and warnings aren't they? It's up to us which. For Matthew this one was both. He didn't listen to its warning, so he learnt its lesson instead.'

'Which was?' Rhian asked quietly.

'To be a bridge, not a barrier.' He turned to meet her eye. 'Matthew should have reached out to Evan, even after what he'd done. And, God knows, he should have reached out to Branwen too.'

Rhian looked out at the river, its eddies picking up scraps of the evening light, swirling glimmers of gold in its dark waters. 'Their son,' she said, still looking away, remembering the cool touch of her father's scar running the length of his arm. 'His name was Gwern wasn't it?'

'Yes,' the old man said softly. 'Yes it was.'

'My father's name,' she said, turning back to face

him. 'How did you know? To find me here?'

'Oh,' the old man said through a sad smile. 'A little bird told me.'

Shifting his weight on the bench he leaned in towards Rhian until his head was level with hers. She saw his hand shaking with strain on the handle of his stick and heard the waver of age in his voice again as he whispered, soft and low into her ear, the sea wind of an Irish accent rising from nowhere through his words. 'Be more of a man than either your grandfather or your father ever were Rhian,' he said. 'Go back to your brothers now. Help them. Be a bridge.'

Ar Lan Y Môr

Ar lan y môr mae rhosys cochion
Ar lan y môr mae lilis gwynion
Ar lan y môr mae 'nghariad inne
Yn cysgu'r nos a chodi'r bore.

Ar lan y môr mae carreg wastad
Lle bûm yn siarad gair â'm cariad
O amgylch hon fe dyf y lili
Ac ambell sbrigyn o rosmari.

Llawn iawn yw'r môr o swnd a chregyn
Llawn yw'r wy o wyn a melyn
Llawn yw'r coed o ddail a blode
Llawn iawn o gariad ydwyf inne.

Ar lan y môr mae cerrig gleision
Ar lan y môr mae blodau'r meibion
Ar lan y môr mae pob rhinwedde
Ar lan y môr mae 'nghariad inne.

Down by the Sea

By the seaside there are red roses
By the seaside there are white lilies
By the seaside is my sweetheart
Sleeping at night and rising in the morning.

By the seaside is a level stone
Where I spoke a word with my love
Around it grows the lily
And an occasional sprig of rosemary.

The sea is full of sand and shells
The egg is full of white and yellow
The wood is full of leaves and flowers
And I am full of love

By the seaside are blue stones
By the seaside are the sons' flowers
By the seaside is every virtue
By the seaside is my sweetheart.

The Second Branch of the *Mabinogion* Branwen, Daughter of Llyr

Bendigeidfran, son of Llyr, is the king of the island of Britain, invested with the crown of London. One day, while sitting at one of his courts in Harlech he sees several beautiful ships approaching from southern Ireland. The ships bear Matholwch, king of Ireland who asks to marry Bendigeidfran's sister, Branwen, daughter of Llyr. Bendigeidfran agrees to the union, but during the celebrations, Bendigeidfran's half-brother, Efnysien, objects and viciously maims Matholwch's horses.

Bendigeidfran offers Matholwch compensation in the form of a magic cauldron that can bring men back to life but without the power of speech.

Matholwch and Branwen go back to Ireland where they are at first welcomed and Branwen has a son, Gwern. But after a year rumours spread about Efnysien's insult and Matholwch has to reject Branwen to stop the uproar. Set to cook for the court, she rears a starling that, after three years, she sends to her brother with a message about her treatment.

Bendigeidfran raises an army that sails to Ireland while he wades, because no ship is big enough for him. The Irish see him coming and retreat over the Liffey, destroying the bridge. But Bendigeidfran makes himself a bridge for his army to cross, and to appease him the Irish build a house, because no house has ever been big enough for him before. But they hide a hundred warriors inside. Efnysien secretly kills the warriors, and when the two sides meet openly peace is restored and Branwen's child Gwern is made king.

Calling Gwern to him, Efnysien throws the child into the fire; fighting immediately breaks out, with the Irish replenishing their ranks by throwing their dead warriors into the cauldron. Seeing this Efnysien repents and throws himself into the cauldron, stretching out to break it and his heart at the same time.

Bendigeidfran, who is wounded with a poison spear in the foot, escapes, as do Branwen and seven men. Branwen dies of a broken heart. Bendigeidfran orders his men to cut off his head and carry it to the Gwynfryn in London to be buried with its face towards France. It was said no oppression could come to the island while the head was in its hiding place.

A brief synopsis: for the full story of the Second Branch see
The Mabinogion, A new translation by Sioned Davies
(Oxford World's Classics, 2007)

Afterword

'Then he went for the horses, and cut their lips to the teeth, and their ears down to their heads, and their tails to their backs; and where he could get a grip on their eyelids, he cut them to the bone. And in that way he maimed the horses, so that they were no good for anything.'

Ever since first reading the *Mabinogion* whenever I've heard the myths mentioned this is the passage that comes to mind. Not a tree half in flame, nor the image of a beautiful woman woven from flowers, nor even the giant Bendigeidfran wading with his army across the Irish sea. But this, Efnysien's mutilation of Matholwch's horses; a brother's disproportionate, displaced revenge for his sister's marriage to their owner.

Why should this passage, more than any other, have made such an indelible mark? I'm sure it's partly because of the quality of the writing – the mythic prose that describes the action so coolly while also hitting all the right triggers. When Efnysien cuts 'their lips to the teeth', the horses' sudden macabre grins are slashed across our vision. We see and feel the panicked struggle in that almost casual aside, 'where he could get a grip on their eyelids'. And then there's that terrible repeated reduction – 'to the teeth... down to their heads... to their backs... to the bone'.

For me, though, this already powerful description was made even more penetrative by a strong personal association with horses. I'd been lucky enough to grow up among them, on visits to my grandfather's smallholding, and at home in the fields and lanes around my parents' house in South Wales. From an early age I'd been well acquainted with the calmness of their assured weight, the beauty of their movement and the mystery of their ancientness. So when I first read of Efnysien's rageful assault against

Matholwch's stable I felt the injustice of his attack keenly, as if his blade had cut into the horses grazing in the fields outside my window, as much as those of the Irish king's.

Adding further voltage to this general association was the charge of a specific memory. One summer when I was nine or ten years old some horses around our village were abused and maimed in their fields. The idea of what happened to those horses, so inexplicable to a young mind, cast a shadow over those fields that took many months to fade. Several years later, when I read the description of Efnysien's crime that shadow darkened again, not just because the description reminded me of the maimed horses in my village, but also because it evoked so vividly the sense of senselessness I'd felt as a child; the inexplicability of violence meted out upon innocent animals.

In the years since, Matholwch's disfigured horses became something of a mythic touchstone for me, occupying a similar territory as the maids hung by Odysseus on his return to Ithaca. Just like Penelope's maids the horses were the 'collateral damage' of the myth's main protagonists, victims of the quarrels and loves of their masters, their innocence reflecting upon their assailants to further amplify the already gratuitous nature of their crimes.

I suppose it's no surprise, given this history, that I should have turned to the Second Branch of the *Mabinogion* when asked to choose a story for this project. When I did, though, I discovered a very different story from the one I'd remembered. I read it again and again. With each rereading the purpose and core of the myth seemed to shift under my gaze. What, after all, beyond that violent act at its genesis, was Branwen's story about? Was this a Welsh-Irish *Romeo and Juliet*? Star-crossed lovers at the mercy of tribal prejudice? Or was this a tale of a beautfiul woman suffering at the hands of the very men who should have been protecting her? Or was this story not about Branwen at all, but actually a cautionary tale about the cyclical nature of atrocity? A lesson in how violence will beget violence in an ever more terrible spiral of destruction?

Branwen's myth is, of course, all of these; a sur-prisingly subtle and layered tale, the focus of which is defined as much by its contemporary reader as the fourteenth-century storytellers who first shaped and mapped its narrative. It is a myth – a story both of its time and yet timeless, part of its colour being leant by the temporal lens through which it's read. For me, a lens of 2009 brought me zooming in once again upon Efnysien's act of violence and also upon Matholwch's 'reply' to that insult – his own excessive and displaced punishment of Branwen upon the couple's return to Ireland. These beats of the myth struck a strong contemporary note with me, although at first I couldn't work out exactly what that note was. It was something to do with the unreasonableness of these men's actions, the excessive nature of their physical and emotional violence and the nihilistic resonance it left in its wake.

And then I remembered. A friend's cousin who, having come of age with a Croatian militia in the Bosnian conflict, began stabbing his pregnant wife with his penknife while travelling home one night in a taxi. Then there was the brother of another friend, recently returned from Iraq, whose wife had banished him from the house after the sight of his own children, in their comfortable home, with their toys, food and security, had driven him into fits of rage. And then there was the man I'd recently met in a Bridgend prison who, back home after two tours in Afghanistan, responded to a minor insult in the pub with extreme and brutal violence. This was the note I'd heard in the actions of Efnysien and Matholwch: the irrational violence of men suddenly returned from a world of conflict into a world of peace. Men whose internal scales had been imbalanced by sanctioned violence and who, shaped by that experience, had returned home to perpetrate more violence, both physical and emotional, themselves.

In responding to the Branwen myth I knew I didn't want to faithfully hit every beat of the original. I wasn't interested in holding up a mirror, translating every aspect of plot, character and incident into a contemporary setting. At the same time, however, I *was* interested in somehow using the myth's architecture, especially the broader arc of its narrative, and I'd be lying if I didn't admit to a certain ludic pleasure in finding ways for other elements of the original text also to exert pressure upon my tale. The sources of this pressure were sometimes from the myth itself – the cauldron that restores dead warriors to life without their speech, the starling that carries Branwen's message home to Wales. Other influences, however, were drawn from the myth's wider orbit, such as the tradition of oral storytelling that lies at the genesis of the *Mabinogion*, or the interpretation of Bendigeidfran as an early prototype for the Fisher King. The greatest influence upon my own story, though, would grow from a seed sown at the very end of the original myth.

'Then Bendigeidfran ordered his head to be cut off. 'And take my head,' he said, 'and carry it to the Gwynfryn in London, and bury it with its face towards France.'

As long as Bendigeidfran's head was concealed within the Gwynfryn in London, 'no oppression' the myth tells us, 'would ever come across the sea' to the island of Britain.

The Gwynfryn (White Hill) is the site of the Tower of London. Given the translation of Bendigeidfran's name as Blessed Crow or Magnificent Crow, these lines from the myth of Branwen immediately put me in mind of the well-known superstition about the Tower ravens. Should the birds ever leave, the superstition runs, the kingdom of Britain will fall. It was while I was researching this superstition further that I came across a suggestion that, during the Second World War, the Tower had been restocked with new ravens from Wales, allegedly under great secrecy for fear of disturbing a fragile public morale.

The idea of this mission fascinated me. It seemed to form a glittering thread across the centuries, one which ran between an ancient British king and his 1940s wartime equivalent, the latter investing in the myth of the former as a talisman to protect their land. It was then that I realised: here it was, my story – rooted to the original and yet not, a journey that could begin where Branwen's myth ended, at the

Gwynfryn in London, before taking us back to Wales and the echoed world of the *Mabinogion*.

Just like the original myth, I hope that *White Ravens* is a story about many things at once, one being the nature of stories themselves: why and how we tell them, and why and how we use them. I should have known, therefore, that the true story about what happened to the ravens in the Tower of London during WWII, would, in its way, be even more suggestive of a wartime investment in an ancient myth, even as it proved that very same myth to be false. This below is an email I received from Bill Callaghan, a Beefeater at the Tower of London whom I contacted after writing *White Ravens*.

'In late September 1940 three ravens died of stress due to their inability to escape the bombing; the remaining four were sent to a sanctuary in Norfolk under great secrecy. Public mood and morale is a fickle thing and as a mass we British are a superstitious bunch so the propaganda value of such an event would have been pure gold for Goebbels. Not a lot exists about the story, it is my understanding though, that the secrecy was so great that the D notice was not removed until 2004. Compare that with the much more pragmatic Enigma secret which was released into the public domain in 1976!'

Owen Sheers

Acknowledgements

I am indebted to Sioned Davies for her excellent modern translation of the *Mabinogion* (Oxford World's Classics, 2007) which I used as my primary source. I'd also like to thank Penny Thomas at Seren for her judicious eye and patience, Zoe Waldie for her speedy reading of an early draft and Fflur Dafydd and Rebecca Jenkins for their emergency translation advice. Most of this story was written at the window table of Petal Belle café on Sullivan Street, New York – thanks to Lara for supplying the coffee and Huw M for the soundtrack.

NEW STORIES FROM THE
MABINOGION

TREZZA AZZOPARDI: THE TIP OF MY TONGUE

Enid wants a dog and she wants to be a spy, but listening in on adult conversations doesn't seem to bring her any nearer to understanding their troubled world. For all that, when times get tough and she has to stay with the Erbins, particularly her rich and spoilt cousin Geraint, she has plenty of verbal ammunition to help her fight her corner.

The original Enid warns her misguided husband of approaching villains, even though he has forbidden her to speak. Trezza Azzopardi's young Enid is also unlikely to respect a gagging order.

RUSSELL CELYN JONES: THE NINTH WAVE

Pwyll, a young Welsh ruler in a post-oil world, finds his inherited status hard to take. And he's never quite sure how he's drawn into murdering his future wife's fiancé, losing his only son and switching beds with the king of the underworld. In this bizarrely upside-down, medieval world of the near future, life is cheap and the surf is amazing; but you need a horse to get home again down the M4.

GWYNETH LEWIS: THE MEAT TREE

A dangerous tale of desire, DNA, incest and flowers plays out within the wreckage of an ancient spaceship in *The Meat Tree*, an absorbing retelling of one of the best-known Welsh myths by prizewinning writer and poet, Gwyneth Lewis.

An elderly investigator and his female apprentice hope to extract the fate of the ship's crew from its antiquated virtual reality game system, but their empirical approach falters as the story tangles with their own imagination.

NEW STORIES FROM THE
MABINOGION

NIALL GRIFFITHS: THE DREAMS OF MAX & RONNIE

There's war and carnage abroad and Iraq-bound squaddie Ronnie is out with his mates 'forgetting what has yet to happen'. He takes something dodgy and falls asleep for three nights in a filthy hovel where he has the strangest of dreams, watching the tattooed tribes of modern Britain surrounding a grinning man playing war games.

Meanwhile gangsta Max is fed up with life in Cardiff nightclub, Rome, and chases a vision of the perfect woman in far-flung parts of his country. As Max loses his heart, his followers fear he's losing his touch.

FFLUR DAFYDD: THE WHITE TRAIL

Life is tough for Cilydd after his heavily pregnant wife vanishes in a supermarket one wintry afternoon. And his private-eye cousin Arthur doesn't appear to be helping much.

The trail leads them to a pigsty, a cliff edge and a bloody warning that Cilydd must never marry again. But eventually the unlikely hero finds himself on a new and dangerous quest – a hunt for the son he never knew, a meeting with a beautiful and mysterious girl, and a glimpse inside the House of the Missing.

HORATIO CLARE: THE PRINCE'S PEN

The Invaders' drones hear all and see all, and England is now a defeated archipelago, but somewhere in the high ground of the far west, insurrection is brewing.

Ludo and Levello, the bandit kings of Wales, call themselves freedom fighters. Levello has the heart and help of Uzma, from Pakistan – the only other country in the free world. Ludo has a secret, lethal if revealed.

NEW STORIES FROM THE
MABINOGION

LLOYD JONES: SEE HOW THEY RUN

Small-minded academic Dr Llwyd McNamara has a grant to research Wales' biggest hero, rugby star Dylan Manawydan Jones – Big M. But as the doctor plays with USB sticks in his office, the gods have other plans...

Llwyd discovers a link between Big M and his own life at the luxurious but strange Hotel Corvo. But from here things only get stranger. Are claims to a link between Big M and the Celtic myths of the past just a load of academic waffle... and what is the significance of the mouse tattoo?

CYNAN JONES: BIRD, BLOOD, SNOW

"No matter how you build them, the world will come crashing against your fences."

Hoping to give him a better start, Peredur's mother takes him from the estates. But when local kids cycle into his life he heads after them, accompanied by the notion of finding Arthur – an absent, imaginary guardian. Used to making up his own worlds, he's something of a joke. Until he seriously maims one of the older kids. And that's when the trouble starts.

TISHANI DOSHI: FOUNTAINVILLE

Gang wars, opium dreams and a mysterious clinic where women are voluntarily confined are all part of the landscape in remote borderland town Fountainville.

But when Owain Knight arrives from across the sea his entanglement with Begum, the owner of the town's mythical fountain, her mobster husband Kedar and her assistant Luna spells a terrible change for them all.

ALSO BY
OWEN SHEERS

THE GOSPEL OF US

'Owen is one of the finest writers at work today. He always finds the sublime in the everyday and the miracle in the mundane.' – Michael Sheen

While the town awaits the arrival of the Company Man, a stranger appears in the windswept dunes, singing songs to the sea. In *The Gospel of Us*, Owen Sheers reimagines his dramatization of *The Passion*: three days of unearthly events in Port Talbot that see the Teacher soothe a suicide bomber and the dead rising from the walls of an underpass.

THE BLUE BOOK

Shortlisted for the Forward Prize for Best First Collection and the 2001 Welsh Book of the Year, *The Blue Book* is a startlingly accomplished début.

'Sheers is a vivid, sensuous writer.' – *The Times*

'It is the truth in the details that suggests indisputably that Owen Sheers is the real thing.'
– Dannie Abse

'He has a knack for capturing the cruelty of life's lack of tidy resolution but, best of all, Sheers has the courage to be tender.' – Francine Stock

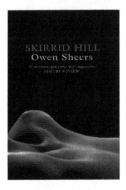

SKIRRID HILL

At once grounded and lyrical, the poems in *Skirrid Hill* reveal the continuing growth of a writer gifted with a rare descriptive power and a uniquely sensitive insight into the trials of life.

'Confident, glittering and suggestive.' – *Poetry Review*

'A gorgeously elegiac volume... beguiling and brilliant.' – *The Guardian*

'Owen Sheers is one of the most exciting new talents around.' – Carol Ann Duffy

SEREN

Well chosen words

Seren is an independent publisher with a wide-ranging list which includes poetry, fiction, biography, art, translation, criticism and history. Many of our books and authors have been on longlists and shortlists for – or won – major literary prizes, among them the Costa Award, the Man Booker, the Desmond Elliott Prize, The Writers' Guild Award, Forward Prize, and TS Eliot Prize.

At the heart of our list is a good story told well or an idea or history presented interestingly or provocatively. We're international in authorship and readership though our roots are here in Wales (Seren means Star in Welsh), where we prove that writers from a small country with an intricate culture have a worldwide relevance.

Our aim is to publish work of the highest literary and artistic merit that also succeeds commercially in a competitive, fast changing environment. You can help us achieve this goal by reading more of our books – available from all good bookshops and increasingly as e-books. You can also buy them at 20% discount from our website, and get monthly updates about forthcoming titles, readings, launches and other news about Seren and the authors we publish.

www.serenbooks.com